Elephant Adventure

A Willard Price Adventure story, about Hal and Roger and their amazing adventures in search of wild animals for the world's zoos.

Hal and Roger are hunting for elephants on the Mountains of the Moon, where flowers grow twenty feet high and there is snow on the equator. They are helped in their search by the Watussi, giants seven to eight feet tall, and the pygmies, who are barely four feet in height, and find themselves involved in the search for the Watussi chief's son Bo, who has been kidnapped by Arab slave traders. While trailing the kidnappers, the boys see a rare white elephant, a prize for which Hal's father has been offered a great deal of money by the Tokyo Zoo ...

D1513604

Willard Price

Elephant Adventure

Illustrated by Pat Marriott

KNIGHT BOOKS
Hodder & Stoughton

To Douglas Claflin

Copyright © 1964 by Willard Price
First published by Jonathan Cape 1964

This edition first published 1969
by Knight Books

Seventh impression 1979

Printed and bound in Great Britain for
Hodder and Stoughton Paperbacks, a
division of Hodder and Stoughton Ltd.,
Mill Road, Dunton Green, Sevenoaks,
Kent (Editorial Office: 47 Bedford
Square, London, WC1 3DP) by
Richard Clay (The Chaucer Press), Ltd., Bungay, Suffolk

ISBN 0 340 04243 5

Contents

Elephant Adventure

1 | Don't argue with an elephant

THE great bull elephant blocked the path.

The boys climbing the steep trail had thought at first that a cloud had covered the sun.

They looked up to find that it was not a cloud that had darkened the sky. It was the black bulk of the largest elephant they had ever seen.

The beast was as surprised as they were. He stopped short and blinked down at them, rumbling angrily, stretching his trunk forward to catch their scent.

His ears had been folded against his shoulders. Now they opened like two enormous umbrellas. They stood out on either side of his fine head as big as table tops. In fact if you made dining tables out of them, eight people could sit at each. Hal estimated their total span, tip to tip, at a good fourteen feet. The beast's deadly tusks, flashing white in the sun, were six feet long.

It was like Hal Hunt to start measuring at a moment like this. His younger brother, Roger, was not so cool.

'Let's get out of here,' he suggested.

'Where to?' The path was solidly walled on both sides by thick brush.

'Back where we came from,' Roger said.

'Won't do any good to run. Then he'd be sure to charge. He can move down this path faster than we can. We'd only get squashed under six tons of elephant – no, closer to seven tons.'

'Will you cut out your figuring,' Roger retorted, 'and do something?'

The bull threw up his trunk and let out a scream that sent the chills up and down the spine and started every bird and monkey within earshot screeching and chattering.

Hal glanced behind. All his black safari boys were huddled in a terrified group fifty feet down trail. All but one. Joro, Hal's chief tracker, stood at his elbow.

In his hands was an elephant gun. He offered it to Hal.

Hal shook his head.

'Let's try to take him alive.'

Joro grinned. He had plenty of courage himself and admired it in others. But to take the bull alive their first job was to stay alive themselves.

They dared not go forward, they dared not go back, and the dense growth that has made the Mountains of the Moon famous closed in on both sides. They might hack their way through it if given time, but it was plain that the great bull would not give them time.

They would cheerfully have dropped through the earth if there had been a hole. There was not.

The only other way was *up*. To escape in that direction was impossible.

Or was it? It took Roger's quick mind to realize that it could be done.

'The lianas,' he cried. They dangled from the branches of every great tree. The equatorial forest was laced with these vines, and their drooping loops, as stout as ships' cables, swung over the path.

'If we could just reach one of those.'

'On my shoulders,' Hal commanded. Roger scrambled up his brother's back, caught a swinging liana and hauled himself aloft. The bull was taken by surprise. He peered in astonishment at these strange gymnastics.

'Quick,' Hal ordered, speaking to Joro. 'Up.'

Joro would have preferred to have his master go first, but there was no time to argue. He slipped his gun into the back straps, and went up, using Hal as a ladder.

The bull was trumpeting savagely and beginning to advance. Joro twisted his foot in a liana loop and hung head downward, stretching a hand to Hal. Hal seized it and was hauled up.

But the bull did not wait to admire this athletic stunt. He got into the act, and fast. Hal felt a blast of hot air up his trouser legs as the beast trumpeted directly beneath him. The boy's ankle was gripped by something soft and strong – the tip of the elephant's trunk.

Joro pulled up, the elephant pulled down. Hal stood a good chance of being torn apart in the middle. Even in that painful moment he saw the funny side of it. He felt himself stretching like a rubber band.

I'll be eight feet tall after this, he thought.

But he knew he would not live to be eight feet tall, nor even his usual six, if the elephant's trunk proved stronger than Joro's arm. Once dragged to the ground, he would either be savagely gored by those sharp tusks, or trampled under huge feet with six – or was it seven? – tons of pressure upon them.

His men came running up the trail, shouting, beating

pans, trying to attract the elephant's attention. The bull screamed back at them.

It was a strange sound to come from so huge a beast. One might expect a roar, not a scream. According to his size, an elephant should thunder like a dozen lions. Instead he screams like an angry woman. A *very* angry woman. Despite its high note, there is so much rage in that scream, it's enough to make one's blood run cold.

So he screamed at the pan-banging safari boys, but he was not to be turned from his purpose.

'One job at a time,' he seemed to say. 'I'll take care of you later.' He kept his grip on Hal's foot, and pulled.

Hal felt something slip above him. The liana that supported Joro had begun to give way. Here was a new danger. If the vine fell, both Hal Hunt and his tracker would end their safari under those terrible feet.

'Let me go,' Hal shouted. 'Loosen up I tell you.'

For once, Joro did not obey orders. His hold tightened on Hal's wrist.

Something else began to slip. Hal's heavy hunting boot strained at its moorings. It was more than ankle-high as protection against snake-bite, and it was laced clear to the top. Either Hal had neglected to lace it tightly that morning, or a lace had snapped under the pull of the trunk wrapped around it – anyhow, Hal was about to lose it.

He had taken great pride in these stout boots, but just now he could think of nothing that would give him more pleasure than to lose one to his tormentor. He tried to contract his foot to let it come off more easily.

It held fast at the heel. Wrenching from side to side eased it a little lower. The laces relaxed. With a final twist, Hal pulled his foot free.

Joro hauled him within reach of the liana, and they both climbed well out of range of the black snake-like trunk.

The elephant attacked the boot. Perhaps he thought it to be a living part of his enemy. He vented his fury upon it, flung it on the ground, stabbed it repeatedly with his tusks, tossed it into his mouth and ground it between molars as big as sledge-hammers, spat it out, trampled it on the stones so roughly that it got ten years' wear in ten seconds.

The seams gave way, the sole broke loose. The stabbing, tearing, flattening went on until nothing was left but a leather rag that no one could possibly imagine had ever been a boot.

Then he buried it.

The boys had often heard of this act but had never before seen it. After an elephant has slaughtered his enemy and is quite sure it is dead, he covers the remains with brush.

Why, no one can say. Who can tell what goes on in his mind?

The elephant is an animal of mixed emotions. He is capable of the wildest fury and the greatest gentleness. He can be generous or jealous, playful or grave, shy or bold, terrific or tender.

He may pay no attention to you as you pass by. But if you block his path, look out. He won't stand for that. Along African roads you see the warning sign:

ELEPHANTS HAVE THE RIGHT OF WAY.

Any other animal may step aside – not so the elephant. He knows his own strength. Why should he give way to anybody or anything?

He is the most powerful mass of muscle on earth. And he has the dignity of a king. Humans look very small to him – even a human in a big car or truck. A blast on the horn does not scare him. Instead, it annoys him, and invites a charge that may mean the end of both human and truck.

And as for a human on foot, he is a mere insect to be swatted as we would swat a mosquito.

But after swatting the animal or man that has opposed him, it may be that his anger turns to pity, and he generously gives his dead enemy a decent burial.

Whatever the reason, he does frequently bury his victim, and now the mountain giant tore out quantities of four-foot-high moss that walled in the path, and did not rest until he had completely covered the sad remains of Hal's boot.

'He'll probably go off now,' Roger said, 'and leave us alone.'

Hal was doubtful. 'I don't think so. You know they say an elephant never forgets. You can be sure he hasn't forgotten us. Anyhow, we don't want him to go off. We must try to get him.'

Roger stared. 'You're out of your head. How could we possibly . . .'

'Hang on!' Hal interrupted. 'Here he comes.'

The bull had not forgotten them. He looked up and came straight for the tree into whose branches they had climbed.

'Let him come,' Roger laughed. 'He can't get us here. Never heard of an elephant climbing a tree.'

'He doesn't need to climb it. He'll just push it over.'

That was a new and unpleasant thought. Roger had seen whole forests laid flat by rampaging elephants. Unable to reach the tender green leaves that grew on top, they butted the trees down.

'But this tree is too big for him.'

'I wouldn't count on it. It's a mopani. Shallow roots. Stick tight!'

Crash!

The great forehead with six or seven tons behind it struck the tree twelve feet above the ground.

The tree shivered like an aspen, and a vervet monkey fell screaming from the upper branches. The bull planted his right forefoot against the trunk and pushed. The tree groaned but remained upright. Again and again he attacked with forehead and foot.

He stopped to think things over. Then he dug his tusks into the ground and pulled up roots. More digging, and up came more roots.

In the meantime, Hal was not idle.

'Toto,' he called. 'The chain!'

The men knew what to do. An elephant is not lassoed like a buffalo or rhino over the head. The trunk and tusks are in the way. A loop of rope or chain is slipped over a rear foot – if and when he raises his foot.

The giant moss had been levelled to the ground by the great feet as if by a steam roller. Over this new path, the men, under Toto's direction, were able to approach the heels of the busy bull. There they waited their chance.

The elephant was butting the tree again, but now with more effect. Its roots broken, the tree swayed dangerously every time it was struck.

The monkeys had long since leaped to other trees. Hal, Roger, and Joro would gladly have done the same, if they could – but they were not monkeys. All they could do was to cling fast and hope they would not be pinned beneath the tree if it fell.

One end of the chain had been fastened around a huge rock. The other end, made into a loop, was placed by the men just behind the elephant's right rear foot. The beast, attacking the tree, was shuffling forward and backward. Surely at some moment he would step into the loop.

The men crowded close behind the elephant. Too close, Hal thought. If the animal should wheel round upon them, somebody would be killed.

'Better unlimber your gun,' he said to Joro. 'But don't use it unless you have to.'

Joro swung his heavy double-barrel ·500 into position.

'Let me have it,' said Roger.

Joro looked at Hal. Hal shook his head. This was no gun for a thirteen-year-old.

'Oh, come on, Hal,' pleaded Roger eagerly. Not that he wished to kill elephants, nor anything else. But if this one *had* to be shot, he wanted to do it. 'I've handled that gun before. I can knock over a sardine tin at two hundred yards. Do you think I can't hit an animal as big as a house?'

Hal smiled. He gave Joro a nod and Joro passed the big gun over to Roger. The boy had some trouble balancing it and himself on the branch of a shaking tree.

Suddenly it happened, just as Hal had feared. The elephant, annoyed by the chattering of the men behind him, turned his head and fixed them with an angry red eye. Then he whirled about and charged. The men scattered like leaves before the wind. At the same instant came the explosion of the ·500.

The elephant's legs buckled and he sank to the earth without a sound.

Roger Hunt also was on his way to the earth. The wobbling tree and the kick-back of the big gun were too much for him. Down he went, and if there had been a rock beneath him it might have been badly spattered with his brains.

But he had the luck of the Hunts. On the ground ready to receive him was a mattress four feet thick. It was the giant moss that grows nowhere else on earth so high as in these mountains.

Deep into it he went. Then its thousands of fibres like steel springs tossed him up again. Twice more he bounced before he lay still, breathing hard, scarcely daring to look for fear he would see the elephant towering above him.

When he did look, he saw the great black hulk lying on its side, the men crowding around it, Hal and Joro clambering down out of the tree.

Roger struggled out of the moss and stood by his victim. He looked at it as David must have looked at the dead Goliath.

'Did I really do that?'

Yet he was not proud. Anyone can pull a trigger, he thought. He and his friends had failed to do what they had set out to do – take the great beast alive.

Hal was examining a rusty spearpoint in the beast's shoulder. The wound was festering.

'That's one thing that made him so irritable,' he said. 'It must have given him a lot of pain.'

'Where did I hit him?' Roger wondered.

'Right here,' Hal said, pointing to a hole high in the skull.

Hal and Joro then did a strange thing. They stooped, took the loop of chain, slipped it over the elephant's foot, and locked it tight.

Roger was puzzled. 'What's the idea of chaining a dead elephant?'

Hal answered, 'He's not dead.'

'Not dead! A bullet through his brain and he's not dead?'

'I'm sorry to correct you, little brother, but the bullet didn't go through his brain. The top of his head is all bone. You could punch it full of holes and he wouldn't die. The brain is beneath all that, just between his eyes. He's only stunned. He'll be up and around again in a few minutes.'

Roger could see the amusement in the eyes of the men. He felt considerably let down. A great hunter, he was!

Hal was laughing. 'So you see,' he said, 'in spite of your murderous instincts, we're going to get him alive.'

Roger thought bitterly, I just hope you don't. Big brothers were hard to bear. They thought they were *so smart*.

But Hal appeared to be right. A deep sigh welled up out of the black mass, then a groan, and the beast opened his eyes. Everyone moved back to give him room. He looked about in a sort of daze. Then with a blast on his trumpet he staggered to his feet and made for the nearest man. The chain brought him up short.

He backed up and thundered forward again with such force that the chain snapped apart just behind his foot. With the loop still around his ankle, but no chain dragging, he rushed between the startled spectators to the path and down it into the forest, screaming as he went.

'Clank – clank – clank,' the sound grew fainter, the screams died away, and peace descended upon the Mountains of the Moon.

Empty-handed, Hal looked the picture of disappointment. Roger said nothing, but there was a mischievous gleam in his eye. Hal could guess what the kid was thinking:

Well, big brother, I didn't get him – but neither did you. Perhaps that will teach you not to be so cocky.

2 | The Mountains of the Moon

T H E men stood listening, even after the last screams of the elephant had been swallowed up in the forest. Now there was dead silence. They seemed more afraid of the silence than of the screams.

Failure to capture their first elephant was taken as a bad sign. They muttered among themselves.

'They don't want to go on,' Joro told Hal.

'Why not?'

'They say it's a bad place. We shall get nothing here. It's a place of death. They have never seen anything like it.'

Hal, looking about, had to admit it was like a bad dream. He and his men seemed very small among the monsters that towered above them on every side.

The trees were giants and they wore whiskers of moss that made them look like old men – a thousand times bigger than old men, with grey beards that came down to their knees and swung in the cold wind. Among their branches coiled vines like black serpents hundreds of feet long. And huge claws of cloud reached down through the trees and combed the ground, as if some great sky beasts were trying to grab some juicy humans for dinner.

Heavy mists hung all about. They were for ever shifting and changing like grey curtains. Up through the mists loomed the strangest plants in the world. It was like a nightmare. Hal felt like pinching himself to see if he was really awake.

Imagine flowers as high as a house! Near him towered a groundsel. He knew that in America and Europe it grew only as high as his ankle. Here it was four times as tall as a man.

At home its tiny seeds were used to feed the canaries. Here a canary could never swallow the seed, for the seed was bigger than the bird.

At home parsley was a little sprig that you used to decorate a platter of meat. Hal stared at the parsley before him – to hold it the platter would have to be fifteen feet wide.

And those white everlastings! In other lands they were flowers that you would have to stoop to the ground to reach. Here they were out of reach in the other direction. Their blossoms were high above Hal's head.

The heather that in Scotland did not grow higher than your shoulder – here it was a tree forty feet tall.

Ferns that usually did not come above your knee were trees on the slopes of the Mountains of the Moon. Their lacy leaves were twelve feet long.

Buttercups were the size of dinner plates, daisies were larger still, and the modest little violet was here a big, brawny bush. Pretty posies that you would wear in your buttonhole were three feet wide in this dizzy Disneyland of monsters.

And those things like telegraph poles – what could they be? Hal stepped close to look. At first he could hardly believe it. But he was a naturalist, already well trained in the study of plants and animals, and he recognized this giant. It was the big brother of the pretty little

lobelia or cardinal flower that he had planted in garden borders at home. There, it was never more than a few inches high – here, thirty feet! Its flower was as big as a barrel.

Roger followed his glance up to the great flower. He looked about at all the other monsters, appearing and disappearing in the driving mist, and he shivered.

'It gives me the creeps,' he said. 'What makes everything grow so big?'

'No one knows exactly,' Hal said. 'Of course it's right on the Equator. So there's no winter. Plants grow every day of the year. They can never rest. And it rains, or at least drizzles, day and night all year long. Then there's something about the soil – it's very acid, and the strong ultra violet light . . .'

'Never mind,' said Roger who was getting bogged down in these scientific details. 'All I know is I would never have believed it if I hadn't seen it. And the animals – are they big too?'

'Well, you saw what a whopper that elephant was. And the gorilla here is the biggest in Africa. The leopards are as large as tigers. And the birds – well – look at that humming-bird.'

It was hovering above the lobelia flower.

'Humming-bird, my eye!' said Roger.

It was as big as a pigeon. But a pigeon couldn't stand still in the air, and pigeons didn't have long bills and poke them deep into flowers. Yes, it was a humming-bird and no mistake.

Roger kicked the mud under their feet.

'Next you'll be telling me that the earthworms are as big as snakes.'

'Exactly,' agreed Hal. 'If we had time to dig down into this muck we'd probably find them. A National Geographic Society expedition found earthworms three feet long.'[1]

'Why don't we hear more about this crazy place? Who's been keeping it a secret?'

'It's no secret. If you look on the map, you'll see it's not far from Lake Victoria, and lots of tourists go *there*. On the map this is called Ruwenzori. That means The Rainmaker. But with all this rain, it's hardly a tourist resort. In fact most people never see it because it's hidden

---

[1] For a scientific report of the monstrous growths of the Mountains of the Moon, see the *National Geographic Magazine* for March 1962.

by rain clouds most of the time.'

'Ruwenzori. I thought its name was Mountains of the Moon.'

'That's another name for it.'

'A newfangled name?'

'No. An oldfangled one. The ancient Egyptians knew about it. They gave it that name.'

'Why?'

'Perhaps because it's so strange. Nothing else like it on earth. It's another world. So on the old, old maps it's *Lunae Montes*, Mountains of the Moon. Funny thing – it was on the map for more than a thousand years – then it was wiped off. Because people decided there was no such place. Explorers couldn't find it. Stanley – the man who found Livingstone – said he had sailed a boat right through the spot where the Mountains of the Moon were supposed to be, and he was sure the mountains did not exist. So they were taken off the maps. But later he came again to this part of Africa and suddenly for a few moments the clouds rolled away and there they were, some of the tallest mountains in all Africa, covered with eternal snow. So back they went on the maps, with a new name.'

'I like the old name better,' Roger said. 'Mountains of the Moon. Sounds weird. And this is the weirdest place I ever saw.'

The men were grouped closely together, still arguing whether to go on or to go back.

Roger became impatient.

'Are we going to hang around here all day? Why don't you tell them to get going?'

'Let them talk it out,' Hal said. 'You can't push an African. He has to make up his own mind. Don't forget, they find all this pretty scary. An African thinks every bush and rock has an evil spirit in it. And the bigger the thing is, the bigger the spook that lives in it. They've got to get used to these giants and find that they won't really hurt them.'

He picked up the tattered rag of leather that once was his boot. He called to a man who was carrying a pack on his back.

'Mali, I think you have another pair of my boots in your pack.'

The boots were found and Hal put them on. He was about to throw the old footgear away when Mali said:

'Let me have those, *bwana* [master].' He was wearing a pair of sandals made from old rubber tyres. He took them off, put Hal's good boot on one foot and tied the leather scrap on to his other foot with pieces of vine. Then he tramped around proudly, for these were the best boots he had ever owned.

3 | The tallest men on earth

THEY seemed to give him new courage. Laughing, he started up the mountain. But suddenly he stopped and stared, for a ghost was coming down the trail.

He could not see it clearly because the mists were swirling around it. It must be a ghost, he thought, for no living man could be so tall. The other men had also seen it by this time, and were jabbering excitedly.

Then the fingers of fog drew away, and it was plain that this was truly a man and no ghost. But the safari men had never seen anyone so tall.

They came from Uganda where few people stand over five feet. They had never before seen one of the Watussi, the tallest people on earth, who live in Ruanda and the mountains. This giant was between seven and eight feet tall.

The Watussi are not Negroes. Nor are they white. Their skin is a rich copper colour. They hold their heads high and they move like the wind. They are marvellous dancers and skilled in the high jump.

'Straight out of King Solomon's Mines,' said Hal. Roger nodded. They both remembered that film and the amazing dances of the Watussi giants.

The figure coming down the trail was draped in a white robe and carried a long staff. He must have been surprised to see these strangers, but he showed no fear.

The Watussi fear no man shorter than they are. And since there are no people on earth taller, they fear no one. Or if they ever have fear, they refuse to show it, for they have the dignity of kings.

The figure in white kept coming, bowed slightly, and would have passed on down the trail if Hal had not spoken.

'Joro,' Hal said, 'ask him to wait. I should like to speak to him.'

Every African tribe has its own language. Joro did not know the language of the Watussi. So he spoke in Swahili, which is a common language known by most East and Central Africans no matter what their tribe.

The tall man understood, but he did not reply in Swahili. Instead he turned to Hal and said in perfect English:

'Is there some way I can serve you?'

'But you speak English!' Hal said in surprise.

The proud copper face relaxed in a smile as it looked down upon the little six-foot white man.

'A few of us know it,' he said. 'We had to learn it when we acted in your talking pictures.'

'You took part in the dances?'

'I did. And in the high jump.'

Roger could not refrain from asking, 'Wasn't that trick photography? I mean – can you really jump that high?'

'Roger,' Hal spoke sharply. 'You are not very polite. We don't even know the gentleman's name.'

But the Watussi had not taken offence. He smiled more broadly.

'It is all right. My name is Mumbo. I am chief.'

Hal introduced Roger, Joro, and himself.

'I don't know what difference knowing each other's

names makes,' Roger said with a side glance at Hal. 'But now that we know them, could he tell us about the jumping?'

'Please excuse him,' Hal said. 'He's a persistent young rascal.'

'That is good,' replied Mumbo. 'He is wise not to believe too much in pictures, nor in words. I think I will have to show him.' He turned to Roger. 'What would you like to have me do?'

Roger thought a moment. He was not going to let this big fellow off easily. He looked up at his tall brother. Then he said to Mumbo:

'Could you jump over my brother's head?'

Hal was not pleased with the idea. 'Think what you're saying. If he doesn't quite clear me, he'll kick me in the face.'

'Sure,' replied the young mischief-maker. 'I thought of that. It would add to the fun, eh what?'

Chief Mumbo put an end to the argument. 'If you will let the boy sit on your shoulders,' he said to Hal, 'I will try to jump over you both.'

Hal stooped. Roger rather unwillingly climbed to Hal's shoulders and sat down, his legs straddling Hal's neck. Hal straightened up.

Now it was Roger who would get those big feet in his face if the chief did not jump high enough. And so high a jump seemed quite impossible. He didn't quite like this turn of events.

He heard Hal chuckling.

'How are things up there?' Hal inquired. 'Comfortable?'

'You son of a gun,' Roger retorted. 'I'll get you for this.'

Hal laughed. 'Perhaps you won't live to get me. Well, we all have to go some time. Goodbye, little brother. It's been nice knowing you.'

Roger, steadying himself by hanging on to Hal's hair, gave it a good yank.

'Ow!' exclaimed Hal. 'What's that for?'

'Just to let you know there's still some life up here.'

Mumbo flung off his white robe. His long slender body gleamed like a copper column.

The boys expected he would go back some distance, then come in a running high jump. But he remained standing within a few feet of them. Suddenly he bent his knees, straightened them again, and was soaring through the air like a kite. Up he went over Hal's head, then over Roger's. As he passed over Roger's head it seemed certain that those big bare horny feet would smash into the boy's face, and Roger tightly closed his eyes.

He felt nothing but a whiff of air as the feet sailed over him. He opened his eyes and looked back. The chief was standing behind him, smiling, not even breathing heavily after his violent exertion. He picked up his robe and put it on.

'Again let me ask,' he said, 'can I do anything to help you?'

'I am sure you can,' Hal replied. 'First let me explain why we are here. Our father is John Hunt. He is an animal collector, and we help him. Our work is to capture animals alive and ship them to zoos, menageries, circuses, film companies, and such all over the world.'

'And your father – is he with you?'

'No. He has had to return to New York.'

'But this is dangerous business – now you must carry it on alone?'

'Not alone,' Hal said. 'We have thirty men. They are Africans, they know Africa, and they know the ways of wild animals.'

The chief shook his head.

'Africans know how to kill,' he said. 'They don't know how to take animals alive.'

'These men have learned how,' Hal said. 'While our father was here we took quite a few animals – giraffes, buffaloes, hyenas, leopards, baboons, a hippo, a python, wart-hogs, bush-babies, honey badgers, and a lot more.'[1]

'You have done well. You have taken everything.'

'No – we must still take the greatest.'

'The greatest? Ah – you must mean the elephant.'

'Yes, the elephant. In fact we want several elephants.'

'And have you taken one yet?'

'No,' Hal admitted. 'We nearly had one – but he got away.'

The chief smiled. 'I fear you will take no elephants here.'

'Why not?'

'Because they are so large and strong. There is no animal on earth so powerful as the elephant of the Mountains of the Moon. And I will tell you the reason for this. The elephants – they truly *are* mountains.'

He looked about at the mountains appearing and disappearing in the ever drifting mists, and for the first time Hal saw fear in his eyes.

'This is no ordinary place,' went on the chief. 'There is magic here. Things are not what they seem. You will think what I have to say is foolish. But our witch doctors tell us it is so and I believe it is so. This land is sacred to the elephant. The mists cover the mountains and then an

[1] The story of this hunt is told in *African Adventure*.

elephant stands before you. The elephant vanishes in the mist, and there again is the mountain. Who can fail to believe that the elephant and the mountain are one? And you who think to match your little strength against an elephant – you might as well wrestle with a mountain.'

Strange ideas, thought Hal, looking about at the mists swirling around the giant flowers and snaky coils of vine as fat as pythons – but who wouldn't have strange ideas in this world of monsters?

'Then you think if we try to take an elephant it will change into a mountain?'

'I cannot say. The white man's magic may be different from ours. But do not ask us to help you take an elephant.'

'Very well,' agreed Hal. 'But there is something else you may be able to do for us.' He pointed to the group of men huddled together arguing in loud tones. 'Our men are afraid to go on. Could you speak to them? Perhaps you can tell them that it is safe.'

'I cannot tell them it is safe because it is not safe. Especially if you are going after elephants. You are walking into the jaws of death. These mountains will close in upon you and trample you under foot. The evil spirits that live in these things' – he waved his hand towards the monstrous plants round about – 'will turn into wild animals and devour you.'

Hal could not help smiling at the chief's superstitious dread, but he replied politely:

'Suppose you let us worry about that. You need not tell them it is safe. But perhaps you will be so good as to tell them where there is a good place to camp.'

'Ah, yes – that I will do with pleasure. You will do us the honour to camp at our village. It is not far. But where

are your men? There are only a dozen here and you say
you have thirty.'

'This is just a scouting party,' Hal explained. 'We
came ahead on foot to explore the trail and see if it is
good enough for motor cars. The other men are down at
the foot of the mountain with our jeeps and Land-Rovers.
They will drive up at once if we send down a messenger
to tell them it is all right. But if our men turn back now
it will spoil the whole plan.'

'I will see what I can do,' said Chief Mumbo, and he
walked over to the group of shivering, terrified men.
The group opened to receive him, and the men listened
respectfully as he told them in Swahili that they would be
most welcome as guests in his village just a little farther
up the trail. They cheered up at once, and the march up
the mountain was resumed.

There were more monsters, but the men were not quite
so afraid of them now. They shied away from the man-
high nettles with spikes as long as darning needles. Roger,
with boyish eagerness to get to the village, did not quite
watch where he was going and plunged headlong into
one of these giant pin-cushions. The sharp spikes went
through his bush jacket and heavy safari trousers like a
hot knife through butter, and he came out howling.

'I'm punctured all over,' he cried.

He got little sympathy from his older brother. 'Better
watch where you're going,' Hal suggested. He examined
the sharp, strong needles of the giant nettle and looked
over the path for broken branches. 'If we run over any
of those our tyres will be full of punctures too.'

The chief came back to see what the trouble was. Seeing blood oozing from holes and scratches on Roger's
arms and face he said:

'I am sorry. The claws of the leopard are very sharp.'

'Leopard?' said Roger, puzzled.

'When a leopard dies it becomes this,' said Mumbo. 'When this dies it becomes a leopard.'

Hal stared. How could this intelligent chief believe such things?

'And these other great things,' he said. 'Are they all wild beasts in a new form?'

'Not all,' said Mumbo. 'Some are the spirits of our ancestors.'

'Then they are nothing to be afraid of,' Hal said. 'Your ancestors were probably good and kind.'

'Ah, yes,' agreed the chief. 'Good and kind. But after death they become bad and cruel.'

'Why should they?'

'Because we do not bring them food. We cannot. There are too many of them. The ones who do not get food become our enemies and seek revenge upon us. They lie in wait for us with sharp claws, they make us sick with poisonous juices, they fall upon us and crush us to the earth.'

As if to show what the chief meant, a flower fell from a lobelia. A man beneath jumped just in time to escape being hit.

Hal stooped down to examine the flower. It was a great blue mass with petals like steel plates. It was as big as a teenage boy, and so heavy that Hal could hardly lift it.

'A very interesting specimen,' Hal said. 'I think I'd like to keep that. Joro, get two of the men to carry it.'

The chief raised his hand. 'No, no – I beg of you. Leave it alone. It would be death to carry it. Unless you wish to lose two men, let it lie.'

Roger whispered to Hal, 'He's nuts. Let's carry it ourselves – you and I.'

'No,' Hal said. 'That would offend him. He's the chief – we must respect his opinion, or pretend to.'

With his foot he rolled the barrel-like flower to one side of the road. 'We'll just leave it there. One of the trucks can pick it up later.'

New wonders appeared as they climbed towards the village. Besides the moss that stood four feet high, there was moss eighteen inches deep on the trunks of trees. Owls had made holes in it and set up house inside. In very wet places the trees were completely smothered in moss – trunk, branches, and all – so there were no trees to be seen, but only great towers of moss. Many of these towers were plastered with gorgeous orchids – red, pink, blue, green, all the colours of the rainbow.

Then there were no trees for a while, but only grass. But what grass! It reached far above the men's heads.

Again the scene changed and they passed among huge banana trees with bananas as big as water-melons. Roger, who liked bananas, found one that had fallen to the ground and slashed it open with his bush knife. He was disappointed, for it contained nothing but large seeds.

Then the chatter of voices could be heard and presently they arrived at the village. Beside the path as it entered the village was something that looked like a doll's house. It was covered with flowers. On a shelf inside were fruits, grains, and bits of meat.

'What does this mean?' Hal asked the chief.

'It is to keep the evil spirits out of the village,' Mumbo explained. 'If we feed them they will not come in and trouble us.'

'And does it work?'

'Not too well,' the chief admitted. 'Some of them still come in. They bring bad luck, they bring sickness, they steal our cattle, they do far worse than all this. They have even begun to take our children. Our boys and our girls – they vanish during the night. In the morning we search for them, through the forest, over the mountains, but we cannot find them. They never come back.'

The chief's face was very sad. 'Our magic has failed us,' he said. 'We do not know what to do. But we must not worry you with our troubles. Welcome to our village.'

It was far better than most African villages. It was clean and neat. The walls of the huts were made of thick moss tied to a bamboo framework with lianas as strong as ropes. The roofs were thatched with stalks of papyrus – the same papyrus from which the Egyptians used to make paper. It would last four times as long as a thatch made of palm leaves. The roofs extended far out over the moss walls to protect them from the rains.

But Hal and Roger were even more interested in the people than in the houses. Men and women seven or more feet tall were walking out to meet the strangers. Their long white robes made them look like marble statues. They surrounded the newcomers and listened to the explanation of their chief who spoke to them in their own language. They smiled down at Hal and Roger, who felt like dwarfs in this company of giants.

4 | The shortest men on earth

B U T not all the people were giants.

Moving around among them were little figures who did not wear white robes – nor anything else except a scrap of bark around their loins. Their skin was not the copper colour of the Watussi, but black.

The most amazing thing about them was their short stature. They stood only three or four feet high.

'It's like something out of *Gulliver's Travels*,' Roger exclaimed. 'You know, where Gulliver meets the little people, and then the giants. Only here they're all mixed in together Who are they, anyhow – these midgets?'

'Pygmies,' Hal said. 'That's the strangest thing about this corner of the Congo. It's the home of the tallest race on earth and the shortest race on earth – the Watussi and the pygmies. Look over there behind the Watussi houses – do you see those little huts that look like bee-hives, about as high as your belt? Those must be the homes of the pygmies.'

The chief had been listening. 'You are right,' he said. 'That part of the village is for the pygmies. They are our servants. But they are an honourable people and worthy of your respect. I wish you to meet their chief, Abu.'

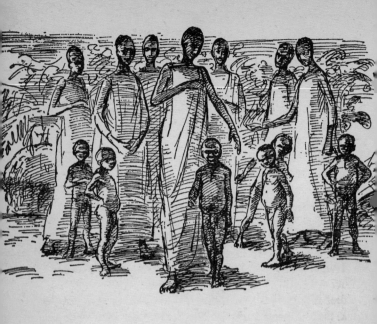

A man no bigger than a large doll stepped out, bowed, and gravely shook hands with Hal and then with Roger. His head seemed too big for his child-sized body, and the deep wrinkles in his face showed that he was an old man.

Hal had felt like a dwarf in the presence of the world's tallest men. Now he felt like a skyscraper as he looked down on the chief of the pygmies. The top of Abu's head was on a level with Hal's hip.

This small bare black creature of the forest with large head and old face seemed more like a chimpanzee than a man. So what was Hal's astonishment when Abu said in English:

'It will be honour to help you. For one year I work

with your people who came to make the pictures that talk. I speak English too good, no?'

Hal smiled. 'If I could speak your language as well as you speak mine, I would be very proud.'

'Chief Mumbo say you come for take elephants. We will help you.'

Hal felt like saying:

'A lot of help *you* would be.'

It was too ridiculous – the idea that these little men the size of eight-year-old boys would be any help against the biggest of all land animals – the biggest animal either on land or in the sea, except the whale.

Tiny little Abu weighed perhaps two stones. What good would he be against a six-and-a-quarter-ton elephant?

Chief Mumbo guessed what he was thinking. 'Do not think that Abu speaks foolishness,' he said. 'The pygmies are the greatest of all elephant hunters. We Watussi are afraid of little, but we are afraid of the elephant. We believe they are mountains, and who can fight a mountain? But the pygmies have a different magic. I still don't believe you will get an elephant – but if anyone can help you, they can.'

Hal still had his doubts, but he bowed again to the black dwarf and said:

'We'll be glad to have your help.'

A messenger was dispatched down the mountain trail, and before night all the thirty men of the expedition and their fourteen trucks, lorries, jeeps, and Land-Rovers were encamped in the great open space beside the village ordinarily kept clear for Watussi dances.

Long-horned cattle, the proudest possession of the Watussi, grazed between the cars and looked with wondering eyes at the tents in which the men were setting up camp-beds and laying out their sleeping-bags in preparation for a cold night. Rain was falling from heavy black clouds.

Hal lay on his camp-bed feeling a bit lost and lonesome. He missed his father. He tried to remember that he was a man now, or almost – nineteen years old, bigger and stronger than his own father, but lacking his experience.

True, this was not the first time the two boys had had to go it alone. It had happened in the Amazon jungle and again in the Pacific islands. But there the sun had shone and the skies were blue and it was good to be alive.

Here it was different. These mountains were the haunt of monsters, giant trees and plants and animals, blinding mists, and baffling mysteries.

The chief said the place was full of evil spirits. Of course the chief was superstitious, but how could you explain the disappearance of cattle, boys, and girls? Perhaps tonight something like this would happen.

Roger in his bed at the other side of the tent was already asleep. Hal would have liked to talk to him, to talk to anybody. He strained his ears to listen. He could hear nothing but the pounding of rain on the tent roof.

Tomorrow he would be going out among the monsters to meet the biggest monster, the elephant. He had already failed on his first try. The chief did not believe he would get one, and Hal was half inclined to agree with him.

The only encouragement had come from little Abu, but it was absurd to think the dwarfs could do anything for him against the king of the forest.

In a deep blue funk he drifted off into a troubled sleep. He dreamed that the little chief suddenly grew as tall as a

tree, picked up elephants between his thumb and fore-
finger, and when Hal asked for the elephants Abu only
laughed with a laugh that shook the mountains, popped
the elephants into his mouth, chewed them up, and spat
out the bones.

5 | Elephants of the sky

HAL woke. The mountains really were shaking. No – it was Roger who was shaking *him*.

'Wake up, you slouch. Don't you know it's morning?'

'Oh, go fly a kite,' Hal mumbled.

For answer, he got a poke in the ribs.

'Wake up. Abu is here.'

Hal sleepily opened his eyes. He half expected to see the Abu of his dream, towering among the stars, munching elephants as if they were peanuts. Instead here was the real Abu, a little wrinkled old man, smaller than Hal's kid brother.

The little chief bowed.

'I will help you get elephants, yes?'

Hal had to admire this tiny creature who was willing to face the greatest animal of Africa.

'It is a good day for elephants,' Abu said.

Hal realized that the rain had stopped. The sun was shining in through the open flap of the tent.

'Hurry up,' Roger insisted. 'Get your duds on and I'll show you something that will make your eyes pop.'

Hal flung on his clothes and followed Roger outside. Roger sometimes exaggerated, but he hadn't exaggerated this time. Hal's eyes popped.

All about him were the giant flowers of this crazy,

hard-to-believe landscape. Behind them towered the
giant forest. Above the forest lay a grey mist. But above
the mist was a city in the sky, white, dazzling, full of
castles, towers, minarets, and spires, all sparkling brilli-
antly in the morning sun.

Hal at first took them to be fantastic white clouds.
Then he realized they were not clouds. They were the
peaks of the Mountains of the Moon.

The mist below them separated from the earth so that
they looked as if they were floating in the sky. They
were so far above that they seemed to belong to another
planet. One could imagine that they were a part of the
moon, or Venus, or Jupiter. Certainly they glowed like
the full moon, sparkled like the stars, seemed as distant
as Heaven itself.

'We're lucky to see them,' he said. 'They're hidden in
clouds most of the year.'

These were the mountains that had been taken off the
map because explorers failed to see them and decided
they did not exist. Now they were on the map, but still
not one traveller in a hundred ever saw them. Even the
natives who lived on their slopes seldom caught a glimpse
of their peaks. And the men of Hal's safari, whose homes
were in Uganda, looked on them for the first time. Their
jaws hung open and they seemed rooted to the spot as
they stared at the white city.

'What makes them so white?' one of them asked. 'Is
it salt?'

'No,' said the wiser Joro. 'It is something they call
snow.'

'What is snow?'

This question stumped Joro. He tried to conceal his
ignorance by saying: 'Don't ask foolish questions.'

But how could people who lived on the Equator know anything about snow?

'You may follow the Equator all the way round the world and find no snow except here and in the Andes,' Hal remarked to Roger.

'But there's enough here,' Roger said, 'to go all the way round.'

Hal plunged into the tent and brought out a map. He studied it, then looked up at the white peaks.

'That's Mount Stanley – named after the fellow who said it didn't exist, then changed his mind. That's Alexandra Peak, that's Albert Peak, and the highest of all is Margherita. There are flocks of other peaks. Nine of them are over sixteen thousand feet.'

'Why are they sticking out their tongues?'

Hal laughed. 'I see what you mean. Those things hanging down that look like tongues are glaciers. They are shown here on the map – Speke Glacier, Elena Glacier, Grant Glacier, and a lot of others. When the glacier crawls far enough down the mountain to get into warmer weather it melts and out from the end of it comes a river. All these rivers help to make the Nile. When it comes to glaciers, these mountains take the cake. There's no such gang of glaciers on the Equator anywhere else, not even in the Andes.'

'You know what they look like?' Roger said suddenly. 'A herd of white elephants.'

Hal laughed. 'You're right. And those things you called tongues – they're the elephants' trunks. Pretty big elephants! Some of those trunks must be five miles long. Now I can understand the Watussi superstition – that the mountains are elephants. And who wouldn't be afraid of elephants that big?'

He looked up again. The elephants of the sky were gone.

As if by magic, they had vanished behind a curtain of mist.

The boys would never see the elephants of heaven again. But they would meet them on earth, and they could never see them without thinking of the sky monsters with trunks five miles long.

6 | Hunters in the tree-tops

SWIFTLY the dark mist spread. Its clammy fingers clawed at the ground. A chill drizzle began to fall.

'I'm afraid the weather has returned to normal.' Hal shivered. 'A good day to stay in bed.'

But Abu and his men did not seem to mind the cold rain on their bare bodies.

'We go now?' said Abu cheerfully.

'We go now,' agreed Hal.

'First you will drink this.' Abu offered a gourd containing a pink liquid. When Hal hesitated, Abu said:

'We always drink this before we go on a hunt.'

'Why?'

'It makes us strong.'

'Then I wouldn't think of taking it away from you,' Hal said. 'You have so many men – you will need it.'

'We have all drunk of it. There is enough left for you and all your men.'

Hal could think of no more excuses. He raised the gourd and took a sip of the strange liquid. It was rather familiar.

'Why, I know that taste. What is it?'

Abu smiled. 'Cola,' he said. 'In your country you must buy it in bottles. Here we don't have to buy it. We pick it off the trees. Big pink nuts – our women boil them and pound them and boil them again. Good, no? Drink it.'

Hal would willingly have thrown out the rather dirty liquid behind a bush, but Abu watched him until he had downed every drop, and all his men had drunk too.

The pygmies had another treat in store for their visitors. They brought a pan of evil-smelling grease and went about smearing the faces and hands of Hal, Roger, and all the crew. Their own bodies were covered with the same stuff and they smelled to high heaven.

'I've had about enough of this,' Roger growled. 'What's the grease for?'

'I think it's elephant fat,' Hal said. 'They put it on to drown the man smell. Then when the elephants catch their scent they think they are just smelling other elephants.'

Roger held his nose. 'I wish I were an elephant,' he said. 'Then I wouldn't mind the smell.'

Abu led the way into the forest. Behind him trooped seventy or more of the little black hunters, and Hal's crew of thirty.

It would be strange indeed, Hal thought, if a hundred men couldn't take one elephant. And yet he had an uneasy feeling that luck was not with him. The vision of those mountainous elephants of the sky stuck in his mind.

Of course he didn't take seriously the Watussi notion that when the mists concealed them they came down into the forest as real elephants. But that monster yesterday – how easily it had outwitted him and his twelve men.

The pygmies slipped along like shadows from tree to tree. They stepped so carefully that no twig snapped beneath their feet. They were completely silent. Frequently they stopped to listen. There was no sound ex-

cept the faraway call of a bird and the 'boom-boom' of a
gorilla.

So the quiet march continued for an hour. Suddenly
Abu stopped and held up his hand. There was a sound
now that did not come from birds or gorillas.

Somewhere up ahead there was a rustling of leaves and
a breaking of branches and the rumbling and snorting of
big beasts. All this noise could not be made by one
elephant.

'Must be a big herd of them,' Hal whispered.

This was more than Roger had bargained for.

'I prefer to take my elephants one at a time,' he said.
'That one yesterday was too much for us. What can we
do with a whole gang of them?'

'Guess we'll just have to trust the pygmies. They seem
to know what they're about.'

Roger was not so sure. 'Are you crazy? Three of those
little runts wouldn't make a good mouthful for an elephant.'

Another signal from Abu. At once all the pygmies
went up the trees like monkeys. With amazing speed they
clambered into the tree-tops.

'They're running away,' whispered Roger. 'Leaving us
in the lurch.'

'I don't think so. They go up there so they can see
better what's ahead.'

Like little Tarzans, the pygmies were swinging along
by the lianas that tied tree to tree. They were moving
towards the sound, trying to get a good look at the herd.
From their high perch they would be able to see how big a
herd it was, whether it was made up of female elephants
and their babies or bull elephants as well, just where they

should attack and what beast they should try to take. Hal and his men followed on foot.

The crackling and rumbling and screaming sounds of the herd grew plainer every moment.

Now the pygmies were pointing and gesturing excitedly. They could see the herd.

At a sign from Abu they swung along from vine to vine, from branch to branch, until they were gathered over the beast he had selected.

They were eighty feet above the animals. If the elephants smelled them, it was only elephant smell because of the elephant grease they had rubbed on their bodies. Even if man smell remained it would not get down to the herd because the breeze would blow it away eighty feet above their heads. Roger had to admit that the little fellows were pretty smart.

It was one of the safari men who gave the game away. He tripped over a root and fell with a thud.

It was nothing compared with the racket made by the feeding elephants. But even when an elephant is making plenty of noise himself he has an ear sharply tuned for any other sound.

At once the breaking of branches and crunching of teeth stopped. There was dead silence in the woods. It is remarkable how noisy an elephant can be when he is feeding – and how silent when he suspects he is being hunted.

The herd began to melt away without a sound. How such huge beasts could move without cracking a twig underfoot had been a mystery to naturalists for years. Finally the secret had been discovered. The sole of an elephant's foot is not a hard hoof. It is soft and elastic. It is full of tiny muscles and delicate nerves. If a sharp stone is underfoot the nerves know it and the muscles make a hollow to fit the stone so it does not hurt the skin. If an elephant loves its keeper it can step on his hand without doing any harm even though the beast weighs many tons. But if it hates its keeper it can flatten that hand until it is as thin as a piece of paper.

When elephants feed, and do not need to be quiet about it, they crush or break every branch they step on. But if they wish to sneak away without being heard they can step on the most brittle twig without breaking it. A man, even barefoot, cannot step as lightly as an elephant, even though the elephant may be a hundred times as heavy as the man.

But the pygmies did not let the herd silently slip away. Down they came from the tree-tops, sliding, swinging, jumping, screaming at the top of their lungs.

It was enough to scare even an elephant. The great beasts spread their enormous ears, threw up their trunks, blasted the air with shrieks of anger and alarm. They milled about in circles. Everywhere they turned little black men danced before their eyes. The elephants tried to swat them with their powerful trunks. But when the trunk swooped down where the pygmy had been, he was no longer there.

7 | Pygmy and porcupine

ONE man was caught. A snaky black trunk went round his body and he was tossed up into the air. The elephant waited to stamp him underfoot as soon as he fell to the ground.

But he did not fall. The astonished elephant looked up. The little black man had caught hold of a branch and swung himself up on top of it. There he sat, laughing at the beast that tried in vain to reach him with its long trunk.

An elephant doesn't like being laughed at. It is almost the only one in the entire animal kingdom intelligent enough to know when it is being laughed at. The beast below the tree trumpeted angrily, and crashed his iron-hard forehead against the tree which, being a young one and not firmly rooted, promptly tumbled to the ground. The elephant poked among the branches in search of his victim. But the pygmy had scrambled out of reach.

Another of the little hunters was not so fortunate. An elephant swung his trunk like a gigantic golf-club and knocked the little fellow spinning through the air above the backs of other elephants to fall at last between two of the huge beasts, where he was squeezed so badly that he lost consciousness. Before he could be trampled upon, other pygmies seized him and carried him to a safe place where a witch doctor was treating those already hurt in the fight.

An elephant can tighten the muscles in his trunk to make it as stiff and hard as a wooden beam. Then he can bring it down on a man or animal with killing force.

A pygmy twice jumped out of the way of a descending trunk. As it was about to come down the third time he saw an ant-bear hole and hopped into it.

He dropped down out of sight and the trunk struck the ground with a terrific blow above his head.

The beast tried to dig out his enemy with his tusks but they failed to reach him. Then he tried his trunk. This was a good eight feet long and circled the neck of the little black. The elephant pulled. There was every chance that he would succeed in hauling the pygmy from the hole and at the same time strangle him with that terrific grip around his throat.

But the pygmy drew his knife and jabbed the point of it into the tip of the trunk.

There are two places where the elephant is very sensitive. One is the sole of his foot, the other is the tip of his trunk.

Snake-bite in either of these two places can kill him. In either place, the prick of a thorn will make him bellow with pain.

Jabbed by the pygmy's knife, the elephant jerked his trunk from the hole and put the tip in his mouth, exactly as a child may do if he hurts his thumb.

But the elephant was not done. More angry that ever, he furiously stamped the ground around the opening into the hole, plugging it tight, and buried his enemy alive.

The pygmy was not worried. He knew his friends would get him out.

What he didn't know was that he was not alone in the hole. The ant-bear who had made it was not at home. But holes made by ant-bears are often used by other creatures – foxes, jackals, honey badgers, snakes, wild-cats, and wart-hogs.

This one happened to be the temporary residence of a porcupine. He was a big fellow and not too good-tempered. He objected to sharing his quarters with a rude stranger who barged in without saying, 'If you please.'

No porcupine can throw his quills. And he cannot puncture you if he comes head on, because all his quills point backward, not forward. But look out if he starts to back up.

This porcupine showed his displeasure at being disturbed by backing up against a portion of the stranger that was as sensitive as the tip of an elephant's trunk. The pygmy howled as several dozen needle-sharp quills punctured his behind.

He began clawing furiously at the earth above him. His friends were already digging for him, and in a few minutes they hauled him out – but what they saw made them rock with laughter.

The pygmy's round rear was just one big pin-cushion stuck with black-and-white pins six inches long.

Still howling, he ran to the first-aid station, where he hollered even louder as the witch doctor pulled out the painful barbs, one by one. Then the pygmy doctor plastered the little fellow's stern with mud and covered it with bark which he tied in place with vines.

In five minutes the pygmy had forgotten his experience and was back in the fight.

The beast the pygmies had selected was a huge female.

'We'll never get it,' Roger said. 'Why, it's bigger than the one yesterday. And we thought that was a giant.'

'Biggest thing I've ever seen on four legs,' Hal agreed. 'It's as tall as a tall man standing on the head of a tall man. And I'll bet it weighs a good twelve tons.'

Roger shook his head. 'I can't believe it. Nothing that walks on land could be that big.'

'Oh, couldn't it? So you've forgotten what you saw at Washington – in the museum. That was even bigger.'[1]

Roger remembered. 'You win,' he said. 'But I'll bet you won't win this elephant.'

'I won't bet on that because I'm afraid you're right,' Hal said, watching little Chief Abu poking the monster with his spear, trying to separate it from the herd. What could this morsel of a man do against this mountain of flesh? It was like a mouse attacking a lion, a squirrel against a grizzly bear. Abu's head came no higher than the elephant's knee.

[1] A mounted specimen of an African elephant on exhibit in the Smithsonian, Washington, D.C., measures thirteen feet two inches at the shoulder and when alive weighed twelve tons.

8 | Buried alive

THEN Hal saw that the little fellow was in trouble.

The chief had turned to give orders to his men. The elephant saw her chance to squash this bothersome mouse. She wheeled about and prepared to sit down on Abu. Elephants have learned from long experience that no animal or man can take that sort of treatment and come out alive.

'Look out!' Hal cried, but he did more than shout. He leaped forward, knocked Abu out from under the subsiding mountain, and sent him spinning twenty feet away.

The little man picked himself up, looked around dizzily, trying to figure out what had happened to him.

Now it was Hal who was in trouble. He had tried to jump clear of the descending bone-crusher and had succeeded – almost. Only his left boot was caught under the great rump. He wrenched and strained, but it was no use. Could he undo the laces? Was he going to lose another boot to an elephant?

But the elephant didn't want the boot – she wanted the whole man. Before Hal could reach for his laces he felt something like a boa-constrictor go round him and squeeze the breath out of him.

The monster stood up, whirled Hal into the air and brought him down with a crash on the ground. There was no moss here to ease his fall. The shock was so great that he promptly fainted. He dreamed that one of those elephants of the sky had fallen on him.

Then the mist cleared from his mind and he realized that he was lying on the ground and the elephant's trunk was feeling him from head to foot. He opened one eye just enough to see what was going on.

Nobody was coming to his rescue. The men stood about, hushed, watching. When Roger tried to run forward to help his brother, Abu stopped him.

Hal understood. The elephant thought he was dead. If anyone rushed in just now, the beast would become excited and really would kill him. Everyone was quiet, and he must remain quiet too.

It was hard to keep still with that gigantic hand running over his body. It was very much like a hand, because the African elephant has two fingers at the tip of its trunk. These are many times stronger than human fingers, as Hal realized when they pulled at his ear and then his nose and jerked up one of his hands and flung it down again. The beast was plainly trying to make sure that its victim was dead.

Hal thought for a moment of making a quick move. Perhaps he could suddenly roll out of reach. But he knew better. The elephant is not as clumsy as it looks. That trunk could move like a flash of lightning, or a tusk could go clean through Hal's body before he had moved an inch. His only chance was to play dead, very dead.

Everybody and everything was as still as a tomb. He squinted again, just long enough to see that not only the men but the elephants as well were standing stock still, all watching this little act.

He was lucky – lucky that this was an elephant that stood over him, not a rhino or buffalo. Those beasts don't

stop when they think their victim is dead. They take out their savage rage upon it, plunge their horns into it, stamp on it, grind it into the dust, tear it limb from limb.

The elephant is not so brutal. It has finer feelings than any other wild animal, finer feelings than any tame animal except perhaps the dog and cat. Some say it has finer feelings than man himself – for no herd of elephants would set out to torture and kill tens of thousands of other beings as man has done more than once during his bloody history.

Hal felt the trunk go round him, and he was lifted into the air. Now he was being carried. He hung as limp as possible and did not open his eyes or show any sign of life.

He guessed what was going to happen. He had read about it many times – elephants are in the habit of burying their dead.

An elephant whose calf has died will carry it in its trunk or on its tusks to a quiet spot in the woods, lay it down tenderly, and cover it with branches and earth. Why, is anybody's guess. Possibly to protect the corpse against attacks by jackals, hyenas, and vultures.

Even its enemy is so treated, for an elephant's anger fades as soon as it has accomplished its purpose.

But what a strange funeral procession this was! Going to the burying-ground wrapped in an elephant's trunk! It was so fantastic that Hal almost smiled. He could hear himself telling his grandchildren, if he ever had any: 'A funny thing happened to me on my way to the grave.'

Now he was being laid on the ground. He was not dropped, nor thrown, but put down very gently on a bed of fallen leaves. The trunk that had gripped him relaxed and was withdrawn.

Now leaves were being brushed over him. They tickled his cheeks and chin and it was hard to keep from screwing up his face. That would be fatal. The elephant's gentleness would change to fury. It would feel that it had been made a fool of and would probably pick Hal up and dash out his brains against a tree. Hal must stay dead to stay alive.

Now twigs and branches were being laid across him. At first it was small stuff, then heavier branches were laid on, and still more heavy. They pressed hard on his face and chest. What was the reason for so much weight? Perhaps to make it impossible for even powerful beasts like the leopard to get at him.

The branches jammed the leaves down upon his face, stopping up his nose and mouth so that it was hard to breathe. How much more of this could he stand without suffocating? Then he would lose consciousness and never regain it. The elephant's kindness would kill him.

Perhaps this business of playing dead could be carried too far. Perhaps he should throw off this load before it became too heavy, before it completely smothered him.

He could not decide. Every moment it was more difficult to get air into his lungs. A deadly sleepiness crept over him. He forgot where he was and felt he was drowning in a deep dark sea and didn't care.

Suddenly he was roused to life by sharp stings on his face and hands, down inside his shirt, and up and down his legs inside his safari trousers.

Even elephants make mistakes. This one had laid its victim on soft leaves, but unseen beneath them was a nest of fire ants. Now they had gone to work on Hal from head to toe. It was just what he needed. His drowsy brain woke up.

How strange that he should have been almost killed by the kindness of the greatest of Africa's creatures, and saved by the anger of one of the smallest.

More bites, hundreds of them. He couldn't bear it. Anything was better than this.

In a spasm of energy he began flinging off leaves and branches. He came out to look into the eyes of a most astonished elephant. He leaped to his feet and began to run as fast as his stiff legs would carry him. The elephant, with a scream that chilled his blood, came thundering after him.

9 | The giant killer

HAL knew it was foolish to run.

Experienced hunters say, 'Never run from an elephant.' The elephant can do twenty-five miles an hour when it has to, and it would take an Olympic sprinter to come anywhere near that.

Or a pygmy. The pygmies can cover the ground at amazing speed. Their light little bodies fairly seem to fly. And it was the pygmies who saved the day for Hal.

Two fast-footed young men overtook the great beast and followed so close on its heels that they were in danger of being kicked into Kingdom Come. Each slashed a hind foot with his knife.

Roger, sprinting along behind, could not imagine what good this would do. A couple of little pokes with a knife could not stop this thundering locomotive.

But the little elephant-hunters knew what they were doing. For hundreds of years the pygmies had stopped elephants in just this way, by cutting the tendons in the hind legs.

The elephant trumpeted with pain, stumbled, and stopped. The hind feet were tipped up on edge. They wobbled helplessly, no longer controlled by the stout tendons like ropes that run down the back of the leg.

The elephant whirled to attack the pygmies, but they nimbly jumped out of the way. They did not need to hurry. The elephant could only stagger slowly after them, dragging its hind feet.

Hal, who had expected to feel the hot breath of the giant down the back of his neck and the point of a sharp tusk between his shoulders, turned to see what was going on.

His first feeling was of relief. But his pleasure turned to bitter disappointment when he saw the prize he had hoped to capture limping and staggering as if mortally wounded.

He came running back to learn what had happened. When he saw the knife-cuts he knew this fine animal would never go to any zoo. In fact it would never go anywhere. It would suffer terrible pain. It would be unable to travel about to get the six hundred pounds of food an elephant must find every day to keep that great factory going. It could not get to a water hole. It would die of thirst, unless it died of starvation.

He felt as sorry for the noble beast as it had felt for him when it believed him dead.

The other men had come on the scene and Abu was among them.

'Why did they do it?' Hal demanded angrily. 'They knew I wanted to take it alive.'

Abu looked at him curiously. 'But they wanted to keep *you* alive. Which was more important?'

Hal was ashamed.

'Of course – they did what they had to do. And I am grateful.' He looked at the suffering beast. 'I wish I could do something for it. But there's no way to stitch up a cut tendon even if the animal would stand still to let me do it. It will have to be put out of its misery. Toto, bring me the gun.'

'Save your powder,' Abu said. 'We will kill it.'

The herd had come close, and now a squealing young elephant came running out to the wounded monster and fondled the big beast with its small trunk, making little sounds of distress and affection. The disabled elephant seemed to find comfort in the presence of the young one and threw its trunk over the small body.

'Must be her baby,' Abu said.

'What will happen to it if we kill its mother?' Roger asked.

That was a question the little chief couldn't answer and he didn't try. He called out a young pygmy spearman.

'He will kill the elephant,' Abu told Hal.

'He alone?'

'Alone.'

'But he is so young,' Hal objected. 'You must have hunters with more experience. And why use only one? You have seventy – why not have all attack together?'

'You don't understand,' the chief said. 'It is a custom of our people. This young man wants to be married. First he must prove that he is a man. He must kill an elephant with no help from anyone. It is our way.'

Hal knew better than to try to interfere with a tribal custom. But it seemed impossible that one boy with a single spear could bring down an enormous elephant.

The young warrior's spear consisted of a broad blade at the end of a bamboo shaft. It was little more than a yard long. To face up to a monster with so small a weapon was like attacking a lion with a darning needle. And the warrior who held the spear was no longer than the spear itself.

A white hunter would not dream of facing an elephant unless he held a gun as heavy as this boy, charged with a big bullet that would plough its way through a stone wall. Even then, it might take many shots to bring the beast down. The bullet might glance off the tough hide or a stout bone.

In fact there were only two places in that great mountain of meat where a bullet would really tell. One was the brain and the other the heart, and the chance of getting through to either one was slim.

As the young brave went forward with his little spear it reminded Hal of David attacking the giant Goliath with a sling-shot.

The elephant pushed her young one aside and turned to face the approaching midget. She tried to frighten him by spreading her ears, throwing up her trunk and screaming like a fire siren. She started towards him, but her hind feet refused to obey. She swung her trunk at him. One blow of that great black club would have killed him. He jumped nimbly out of her way.

He ran round behind her, but she turned to meet him. This wheeling about was something she could do. Again he got behind her. Again she spun around and one of her long tusks scooped into his shoulder, cutting a gash a half-inch deep. It was enough to discourage most hunters – but not the young pygmy.

He was too busy to think about it. Now the baby elephant had joined in the attack. It was a husky baby, weighing a good half-ton. Its tusks were short, but sharp. The boy did his best to keep out of its way.

The other elephants in the herd screamed and trumpeted, and some of the bolder ones attempted to break through the line of pygmies and safari men. If they

succeeded, it would be all up with the little warrior. They could not be held back long. He must act fast.

This time when he ran round behind the big elephant he got unexpected help from the little one. It happened to be in its mother's way when she attempted to whirl about. The split-second delay was just what the pygmy needed.

He ran in between the elephant's hind legs and raised his spear to the big beast's belly. Still running, he ripped a slit six feet long.

This was something a bullet could never do. It could penetrate the soft skin of the belly but it could only make a small hole, then lose itself in the great inside.

This was the famous and traditional pygmy way of killing an elephant. Out from the long cut fell the great stomach and the entire digestive system, including some six hundred pounds of fodder eaten by the beast during the past twenty-four hours. The elephant with a last scream of defiance fell over on her side.

The young elephant-hunter came out smiling. His spear had been broken, his shoulder wounded, and he had been badly kicked by a forefoot as the thrashing elephant fell.

But what did that matter? He was a man now and had a right to marry and make a home.

10 | How to eat an elephant

H E was almost knocked over by a shouting, laughing host of pygmies who came rushing up and scrambled inside the still-living elephant.

Pygmies have to be excused if their table manners are not the best. When they get hungry they cannot drop in at a supermarket. They drop into an elephant. They don't get the chance often. For days, even weeks, they may go hungry. Therefore, when at last the opportunity comes to eat, you can't expect them to be dainty eaters.

Sometimes they cook their meat. More often they can't wait, and eat it raw.

'Why do they go in?' Roger wondered. 'Can't they just chop it up on the outside?'

'They probably will, later,' Hal guessed. 'But the things they like best are inside. Especially the heart. The first ones in are probably pushing their way through right now between the lungs to get at the heart.'

'Is it big enough to bother with?'

'I'll say it is. It's about a foot wide. It weighs more than a pygmy. It's the elephant's motor and it has to be big and strong to run such a large machine. It exerts tons of pressure. Blood comes out of it with the force of water from the hose of a fire engine.'

'It must beat very fast to do that.'

'No, strangely enough, the normal heart-beat is only

about thirty a minute. Pretty slow compared with our seventy to eighty. But about a hundred times as strong.'

'But why do they want it – is it so delicious?'

Abu heard the question. 'It is tough,' he said. 'There are other parts that taste better.'

'Then why are they so keen about eating the heart?'

'The elephant has great courage. We believe that if we eat its heart we get the courage of the elephant.'

Chunks of the heart were now being passed out to those who had been unable to get inside. The chunks were cut into smaller pieces and distributed so that everyone might share the courage of the elephant.

Hal and Roger were not neglected. Scraps of heart still dripping with blood were pressed into their hands. They would have liked to drop these precious gifts in the bushes. But the pygmies were watching them. It would not do to offend them.

'Here goes,' said Hal, and downed the bloody bit of courage. He managed to smile and smack his lips and the pygmies laughed and jumped up and down with pleasure. 'Very good,' Hal said to Abu.

Roger held out his portion. 'Since it's so good, you may have mine too, big brother.'

'Not on your life,' Hal said under his breath. 'If you don't have the courage to eat it, that proves it's just what you need – to give you courage. Down with it!'

Roger downed it and the pygmies danced with delight.

'You eat our food,' Abu smiled. 'Now we feel that you are one of us.'

A man came out carrying two kidneys, each twice as big as his head. These were at once cut up and passed around. Hal and Roger suddenly had business elsewhere and in the general confusion they managed to escape without getting a share.

Great chunks of meat were being handed out and eagerly devoured. With them suddenly came a violent rush of almost clear water.

'Somebody's knife must have slipped,' Hal said, 'and cut open the water stomach.'

'Water stomach? What's that?'

'A special container for water – like a camel's. An elephant drinks fifty gallons of water a day – when it can get it. In the dry season it can't get it – at least not every day. So it has to store water in a special tank. Haven't you heard how hunters dying of thirst kill an elephant to get water? It doesn't taste so awfully good, but it's wet.'

'I think I'd rather go without.'

'Not if you were dying of thirst. And when the elephant gets thirsty and there's no waterhole near by he can use some of the water from his own storage tank. He can drink it, or he can spray it over himself to cool his hide.'

'But how does he get at it?'

'He puts his trunk down his throat and sucks up water into his trunk. The trunk of a big elephant will hold about four gallons. Then he can spray it up into the air so that it falls on his back. Or he can shoot it into the face of an enemy. It comes out with force enough to knock you over. Laugh at an elephant, and you are apt to get soaked.'

Abu said, 'One time we start fire in grass to stop elephant. He put out fire with water and get away.'

'Pretty smart,' Roger agreed. 'Doesn't seem to be much he can't do with that trunk.'

'That's right,' Hal said. 'He feeds himself with it. He can hug or kiss or fight with it. He can pick up a blade of grass or throw a rock weighing a ton. The end of a trunk is as delicate as a girl's fingers or the tongue of a humming-bird. And yet – see those men trying to cut off the trunk – they can hardly get a knife through it, although there is no bone in it anywhere. It's so strong that one swat from it on the side of your head could make you deaf for life – if it didn't crack your skull wide open. In olden times they used to train elephants as Lord High Executioners to crush the skulls of condemned criminals.'

'The trunk is really just the nose, isn't it?'

'Just the nose. But what a nose! There's a story about how the elephant got such a long nose.'

11 | Story of the long nose

'THEY say that once upon a time,' Hal continued, 'elephants had ordinary noses like yours or mine. But one day as an elephant was drinking at the riverside a crocodile stuck his head out of the water, opened his jaws, and seized the elephant by the nose. Then he braced himself and tried to pull the elephant into the water. The elephant pulled back. They were both very strong. The only thing that was not strong was the nose. It began to stretch. It became a foot long, two feet, three feet, four feet, and still the crocodile pulled and so did the elephant. They pulled all day and they pulled all night, and the rising sun looked with astonishment at an elephant with a nose eight feet long.

'But the crocodile was getting tired. Suddenly the elephant gave an extra yank and hauled the crocodile up on to the bank. The crocodile let go and tried to escape into the river. But the elephant killed it with one whack of his new nose.

'Then he went back to join the other members of his herd, but they laughed at his strange appearance and would have nothing to do with him. They went on with their breakfast, kneeling so they could get their mouths down to the grass. The elephant with the long nose didn't have to kneel. He just pulled up some grass with the end of his nose and brought it up to his mouth. There were many leafy branches overhead that looked delicious, but the other elephants couldn't reach them. The elephant with the long nose reached them easily and fed himself and his wife and his family and his best friends.

'They stopped laughing at him. They wanted noses just like his and asked where he had obtained such useful equipment. He recommended the crocodiles. Soon the crocodiles had all the business they could handle, lengthening the nose of every animal in the herd, and when other herds saw the results they came too until all elephants in Africa were supplied with long, powerful, useful trunks. And so it has been ever since.'

The trunk, when it was finally cut off, was brought and laid before Chief Abu who seemed quite delighted to receive it.

'What good is it to him?' Roger asked. He had never seen anything much more unpleasant that this huge black snake smeared with blood.

Before Hal could answer Abu said, 'Much good. Make fine soup. Like, what you call, oxtail, but better. I give you some.'

'I can hardly wait,' Roger said. He planned to be somewhere else when the soup was passed round.

Pygmies swarmed like ants over the great carcass. They chopped and hacked and jabbed and sawed and slashed. Sometimes their knives went through and hurt the men inside, who would scream with anger and push their knives through hoping to puncture someone on the outside.

Two men in the dark interior got into a fight and there was a lot of squealing and the clashing of knives. Soon one of them was chucked out, unconscious, and was carried away to the witch doctor to be treated.

The skin was an inch thick. Every scrap of it was

saved. Some of it would be used to make soup. Some of it, Hal explained, would be dried and made into trays to hold ground corn and other foods.

'But how do you know all these things?' Roger wondered. 'Anybody would think you had grown up with the elephants.'

He often made fun of his elder brother and played tricks on him. But he really had great respect for him. He knew how hard Hal had studied to become a naturalist, devouring scientific books as eagerly as other young men of his age devoured ice cream and cake, determined to learn the habits of animals, their anatomy, their chemistry, what made them tick. But he was modest about it.

'Afraid I have a lot to learn,' he said. 'I have more questions than answers. Tell me, Chief, why did they chip out that hole in the skull?'

'To get the brain.'

'Is that good to eat?'

'Not *taste* good, but *do* good. Eat heart, get courage. Eat brain, get wise. Elephant more wise than any other animal, more wise than pygmy. When we eat brain, we eat wisdom.'

A thirty-pound mass of dripping, squirming wisdom was taken from the elephant's skull. It also was laid before Chief Abu. He must keep it and give a bit to anyone who needed it, so the foolish could become as intelligent as the elephant.

'Wouldn't it be great if it would really work?' Roger said. 'Just what I need in school. Instead of doing homework half the night I'd just take a bite of brain and watch TV.'

The four feet were cut off and cleaned out. They would make fine buckets for the pygmies. Big bones were extracted – they could be used as clubs to fight wars with other tribes or to kill small animals. The great tongue, soft as velvet, was removed entire – it would make a pretty fair bed. Large gobs of fat were preserved. They would be useful in cooking and as fuel for oil lamps. Hairs from the tail would be woven into bracelets.

Other men attacked the great mouth. Each one of the giant's mighty molars weighed some twenty pounds. They would make beautiful building blocks, or they could be hollowed out and used as cups or bowls. Some were very loose and easy to remove.

'They were ready to fall out, anyhow,' Hal said.

'If they were all as loose as that,' Roger said, 'they'd all fall out, and then how would the elephant eat?'

'He would eat,' Hal assured him. 'No tooth falls out until there's a new one underneath ready to take its place. During an elephant's lifetime he loses six complete sets of teeth and grows six new sets.'

'Why should he need so many teeth? I don't.'

'You eat soft foods.'

'So does he. Grass and leaves.'

'It takes a lot more than that to fill him up. He eats bushels of twigs and sticks, branches and bark, and even the solid wood of tree trunks when he can't get anything else. And he spends about twenty hours out of every twenty-four eating. So he grinds his teeth down pretty fast and he has no dentist to give him a set of dentures. But Nature takes care of him, so even if he lives to be a hundred years old he still has a good set of teeth in his head.'

Now the men were trying to loosen the great ivory tusks. They were nine feet long and each must have weighed more than one hundred and fifty pounds.

'Who gets the tusks?' Roger asked. 'The chief?'

'Please,' Chief Abu objected, bowing to both boys most politely. 'You will accept the tusks.'

'But,' Hal said, 'they are the best part. You could sell them for much money.'

'Money? The pygmies do not use money. Why do we need money? The forest gives us everything we need.'

'Those tusks are the greatest,' Roger said. 'I'll bet they're just about a record.'

'They could be a record these days because most of the big elephants have been killed off. But there used to be plenty of ivory this big or bigger. The heaviest tusk in existence is in the British Museum. It weighs two hundred and twenty pounds. The record length of tusk is eleven feet, five and a half inches. Just imagine how you would look with two teeth eleven feet long.'

'But these aren't teeth. They're tusks.'

'We call them tusks just to distinguish them from the other teeth. But they are actually teeth – the incisors – exactly the same as the incisors in your own mouth but about four hundred times as long.'

'There's something screwy about all this,' Roger complained as he watched the baby elephant fondling the great carcass. 'I thought this was the baby's mother. But it can't be. Female elephants don't have tusks.'

'You're getting your signals mixed. You're thinking of the Indian elephant.'

'Well, what's the difference?'

'All the difference in the world. The African is four feet taller and twice as heavy. Its head is held high, not slumped down like the Indian's. Its ears are three times as wide and stand out like the black sails of a pirate ship. The tusks are twice as big and both papa and mama have them. The African has two nubbins at the end of its trunk like a finger and thumb and can pick things between them. The Indian has only one nubbin and is not nearly as skilful. The African is a more magnificent brute in every way.'

'If it's so fine, why don't they use it in the circuses?'

'Because it's a wild animal. It might break loose and kill people. The Indian elephant is easily tamed. It will take orders. The African gives orders. A zoo will take an African because it can be kept behind bars. A circus must have an animal that's safe. The Indian walks down the main street in a circus parade as meek as a kitten. The African would be snorting and bellowing and rampaging through the crowd into shop windows. The Indian will quietly take a peanut from your hand. Offer the African a peanut and he's just as likely to twist off your head. Another reason why the circus doesn't use the African – it costs twice as much. The circus can get a good Indian elephant for less than five thousand dollars but an African will cost ten thousand.'

'You mean to tell me we lost Dad ten thousand dollars by not taking this one alive?'

'You guessed it.'

Both boys were gloomily silent for a time. Roger said:

'I had no idea they were worth so much.'

'Oh, that's not the half of it. We have an order from the Tokyo Zoo for a white elephant. They would pay fifty thousand dollars for it. Of course, our chance of getting a white is about one in a thousand. Looks as if we can't even get a black.'

Roger shook his head mournfully.

'I think the Mountains of the Moon have us jinxed.'

But he cheered up considerably when the mighty tusks were finally dug free and laid down before him and Hal. They were beautiful, and valuable, a real prize. Hal made a little speech of thanks to Chief Abu.

The men were not quite done with the tusks. Inside each was a nerve. It must be removed or it would rot and spoil the tusk.

Out it came, a long spongy thing like bright red jelly, as thick through as a man at one end but dwindling at the other to a tip no larger than the point of a pencil.

'And all that is just a nerve?' Roger marvelled. 'Wow, what a toothache, if anything got the matter with that!'

'You're not kidding. If it's injured by a bullet, or in any other way, the beast may go crazy with pain.'

'Well, I suppose our little friends will gobble it up because they figure it will give them nerve.'

'Just the contrary. They won't touch it because they think it will give them the elephant's toothache. And an elephant-size toothache in a pygmy-size mouth would be just too awful.'

'Of course that's just superstition.'

'Well, I suppose so. But there must be something strange about that nerve. The dogs won't eat it either. Even the flies won't settle on it.'

It seemed to be true. Roger noticed that flies swarmed over the carcass but not one lit on the juicy red nerves extracted from the giant's teeth. It was just one of the unexplained mysteries of this mysterious continent.

Only the skeleton of the great beast was left. You could look through the bare ribs and see the naked little men still trying to scrape some last bits of meat from the bones.

'They're like squirrels in a cage,' Roger said.

'Or like prisoners behind bars,' Hal added. 'It would make a good jail – if pygmies ever needed a jail.'

Chief Abu shook his head.

'If one of our people does wrong,' he said, 'we don't put him in jail. He would like that too much. We would have to feed him and he would not have to do any work. It is too hard to get food. We cannot spare food for the bad man.'

'Then what do you do with him?'

'We turn him over to our witch doctor. He puts a curse on him and gives him a bitter drink. He dies.'

'Aren't you pretty hard on him?' Roger objected.

The question seemed to surprise the chief.

'Hard? Yes, we are hard. Life in the jungle is hard. Once in a moon or two moons we kill an elephant and everybody eats. In two days the food is gone, hunger returns. You know what it is like? To be hungry? No, you do not know. In your country there is much food – plenty for good men and bad men. You can afford bad men. We cannot.'

Hal nodded. It was a hard life, he thought, not only for the pygmies but for all Africans. It wasn't just hunger. There was war, too. Fighting was going on a thousand miles away in the southern part of the Congo. No trouble yet in the Mountains of the Moon, but who could tell when it might come?

12 | Roger becomes a mother

THE baby elephant whined and whimpered about the cage of bones that was all that was left of its mother.

It stroked the bare ribs with its little trunk. It nudged and pushed with its forehead, making questioning noises as if to say: 'Why don't you get up and give me my dinner?'

It searched for the comforting sources of fresh warm milk and found nothing but more bones.

In a fit of anger it whacked the skeleton with its trunk and poked it with its small tusks, squealing with baby rage. When this didn't work it turned gentle once more and petted the great skull with a touch as light as a butterfly's. It groped for the trunk and was plainly distressed not to find it, for it is with the trunk that the elephant kisses and embraces and protects its young.

'Poor little duffer,' Roger said, and started towards the small elephant.

'No, no,' cried Abu. 'Little one big trouble, quick.'

'I suppose he's trying to tell you,' Hal said, 'that the little one is badly upset and might hurt you.'

'I'll take a chance,' Roger said.

'Remember,' Hal warned him, 'that's a half-ton baby you're fooling with. If he knocks you down and steps on your face you won't look very pretty in your coffin. His tusks may be only two feet long, but that's long enough to go right through you and come out the other side. Have a care, young man.'

When Roger reached the young elephant's side he was surprised to find how big it was. From a distance it had looked very small in comparison with its giant mother.

But it wasn't such a little fellow after all. It stood as high as Roger and was heavy enough to make ten Rogers.

Those tusks looked uncomfortably sharp. The trunk which had seemed so small was a yard long and Roger knew it could pack a wallop as hard as a prize-fighter's punch. The baby's feet were as big as boxing gloves – with more power behind them than any boxing glove ever had.

The big baby wheeled about and made a rush at Roger. The boy stood his ground. When the elephant stopped, his tusks were not two feet from Roger's face. Roger tried not to show fear, but his heart was beating fast.

He spoke soothingly. 'Now, now, little fellow, nobody's going to hurt you. You need a mama. How about me?'

The young animal did not seem to know what to do next. His instinct was to defend himself and to defend his mother. But he was afraid of this strange animal on two legs.

Finally he plucked up courage to attack, blew a blast on his little trumpet, waved his little trunk in a wobbling circle and gave Roger such a swat on the shoulder that the boy fell flat on the ground.

Hal would have run to help him but Roger signed to him to keep away.

He knew very well that he might be trampled. But some instinct told him to stay where he was. He remembered in a flash a boy he had once feared and fought and knocked down. As soon as he had knocked him down he didn't fear him any more and only wanted to make friends.

It might work with this intelligent animal. Surely the elephant could not be afraid of him so long as he lay flat and helpless.

The elephant raised a boxing-glove forefoot and prepared to give his victim a half-ton push in the face. Roger controlled his wild impulse to roll to one side. The big foot hovered over him, then was replaced on the ground.

The black trunk with its pink two-fingered tip explored his face and chest.

Roger kept on murmuring sweet nothings in a low tone.

Then he slowly raised his hand and touched the little trunk. It was sharply pulled out of the way. But after a moment it came back and continued its exploration. It ran under his bush coat and into his pockets.

Roger again raised his hand and placed it ever so softly on the exploring trunk. There he let it rest quietly for a moment. Then he began tenderly stroking the trunk.

He knew that elephants receive affection and give affection by means of the trunk. They stroke each other with the trunk. Two friends will coil their trunks together and so stand for a long time giving and getting comfort. The first thing the baby feels upon entering the world is the touch of a mother's trunk. The sick animal is caressed by his friends, who wave the vultures away and sprinkle him with cooling water and place mud on his wounds –

and all is done with the trunk. The last sensation of the dying elephant, if he is loved by the herd, is the gentle touch of trunks.

The baby elephant stopped its search and stood perfectly still, eyes fixed upon Roger, as if trying to decide whether he should accept such familiarity from a perfect stranger.

Then he snorted, pulled away, and went back to his mother. But there was no comfort to be found here. After petting the dead bones, the little beast stood swaying from side to side, swinging his trunk back and forth, while tears trickled from his eyes. For the elephant is one of the few animals that actually weep.

Roger cautiously got to his feet. For a little while he stood perfectly still. Then he began to talk – softly. The elephant would understand, not his words, but the tone in which they were spoken.

Roger ventured again to stroke the trunk. Then he went on to the big floppy ears. He scratched behind the ears where they join the body. His hand went on over the neck, along the backbone, down the flanks, stopping to pluck off some of those bothersome ticks. For although the elephant's skin is an inch thick it is full of nerves and the bite of the smallest insect is felt.

The elephant seemed to appreciate these attentions and Roger began to feel that he was winning. But suddenly the trumpeting of the herd distracted the little lost beast. There were his friends – he must go to them.

Away he went in a fast shuffle and the line of men parted to let him through. He reached his aunts and cousins and neighbours and they crowded around him seeming happy to have him back.

Then there was a curious change. The crowd broke

up, the animals wandered away and left the little beast standing alone.

He whimpered his displeasure and followed a large female, perhaps an aunt, but when he came close auntie turned upon him savagely, brandishing her tusks, and scared him away. He tried others of his relatives and old friends, but the effect was the same. They would have nothing to do with him.

'What's got into them?' Roger puzzled. 'They act as if he didn't belong.'

'He doesn't,' Hal said. 'You fixed that.'

'Me? What did I do?'

'You petted him.'

'What's the harm in that?'

'You smell bad. You made him smell bad.'

'Well I like that,' Roger protested. 'I'll have you know I took a sponge bath all over this morning before we started out. How could I smell so bad?'

He knew his brother was kidding him, but he didn't much care for the joke.

Hal grinned. 'Of course you don't smell so bad to me. I'm used to you. And the baby elephant doesn't mind, because it doesn't know any better. But you can't fool the grown-up elephants.'

Roger said impatiently, 'Will you cut the comedy and tell me what this is all about?'

'Sure, I'll tell you,' Hal said more soberly. 'It's just that elephants hate the smell of man. You can't blame them. They've been attacked by men so much that they either attack or run when they get the man odour. To them it means death, or at least danger. The babies don't know about this, but the adults have become wise and the more trouble they have had with hunters the more they dislike the stink of humans.'

'But I only petted him for a minute or two.'

'That's enough. Elephants have a terrifically keen sense of smell. They can scent a human a mile away, if the wind is right.'

'Seems to me,' Roger grumbled, 'you could have told me all this before I touched the baby.'

'I didn't tell you because I thought you were doing just the right thing. True, the herd won't take the baby back. But we'll take it. Or, rather, you will. You have just become a mother. And I can tell you it's no easy job you've picked for yourself – playing mama and nurse to a baby ten times your size.'

'I don't think I'll have to,' Roger said. 'He's not coming back. He's forgotten that I exist.'

So it seemed. The baby stood apart, facing away from the men and still making plaintive little questioning sounds as if begging the herd to have a heart and take him back.

Then he suddenly whirled about, trumpeted loudly, charged through the line of men and came to a halt beside Roger.

'There you are,' Hal said. 'Now he's really adopted you.'

13 | The trap

'COME. Quick. We catch big one.'

It was Chief Abu speaking. Hal shook his head. He had almost given up hope. Everything had gone wrong. Yesterday the elephant had escaped, taking most of the chain with him. Today – he looked at the mournful pile of bones – they had been unable to take their quarry alive. He could almost agree with Roger – the Mountains of the Moon had them jinxed.

Without much enthusiasm, he followed Abu into the woods. They pushed past ferns thirty feet high with leaves ten to twelve feet long. Heather, lobelias, begonias, pansies, towered around them. Above them rose gigantic trees, and beautiful black-and-white colobus monkeys looked down from the high branches. Far away there was a sound like a sonic boom – it came from the great drum-like chest of a big gorilla.

They came out of the brush on to a narrow path.

'Elephant trail,' Abu said. 'Every day many elephants come here. We catch one – no?'

Hal felt like repeating the 'No.' But he only nodded gloomily.

A number of pygmies were hard at work. Some of Hal's men were helping them. They had dug a hole a foot deep in the path. It was a little larger than the forefoot of an elephant. Now they were laying a loop of rope around the edge of the hole. The other end of the rope was tied round a big log.

Hal had never seen a rope like this one. It was as heavy as the hawser of an ocean liner, perhaps heavier. It was a good five inches in diameter. Where did the pygmies ever get such a rope? He asked Abu.

'It is made of many hides,' Abu said. 'The hides of giraffes, antelopes, hartebeest, rhino, eland, zebra, and buffalo. Our women make it. They scrape the skins and pound them with clubs. They pound them for many weeks. Then they twist them together to make this rope.'

'But is it as good as a chain?'

'It is better. It will stretch – a chain will not. The elephant – he comes. He steps in the hole. When he takes up his foot, the loop is around his ankle. It makes tight. He tries to go on, but the rope is tied to this log. He pulls hard. The rope stretches like what-you-call elastic. It does not break like chain. When he stops pulling to rest, it goes back.'

'Then what happens?'

'He pulls again – harder. So hard, he drags the log behind him.'

'Why don't you tie the rope to a big tree instead of a log? He couldn't drag that away.'

'Then he would break the rope – like chain. But the log, it moves, so the strain on the rope is not too great. You see? We never forget – elephant is king. He is strongest animal in whole world. You do not say no to king, or elephant. You say a little no, a little yes. If you do not let him win a little, he win too much. So the elephant wins a little – he goes on along path. He pulls the log. But it is very hard work. He get very tired. He stop. We catch him.'

'I'll believe it when I see it,' Hal said.

Light sticks were laid across the hole and the loop of rope. Then the trap was entirely covered with leaves. Hal noticed how carefully this job was done. The pygmies did not touch the leaves with their hands or bare feet, but used sticks to rake them into place. Thus they would bury the smell of man.

When the work was done they did not walk back along the path but plunged into the jungle and went round about, coming out finally near the herd and Roger with his big baby.

Now all the men, directed by Abu, went behind the herd and began an unholy racket, shouting, screaming, banging broken branches against tree trunks, throwing stones, making noise in every possible way.

Some of the elephants screamed back and charged. They came up against a wall of spear-points that pricked them in all tender parts, including the sensitive trunk. The hundred prancing, shrieking devils were too much for them. They turned and followed the rest of the herd towards the forest. Soon they were treading along the elephant trail, in single file.

Again Abu led Hal round about to the point in the trail where the trap lay concealed. They stopped behind some thick bushes where they could see and not be seen.

Hal still doubted that the plan would work. He doubted even more when he saw the first animal in the line. It was a scruffy beast with a ragged hide, and he was sure no zoo would want it. But it was the one that was going to be caught in the trap.

The elephant came on with long, lazy strides. It seemed sleepy, or was it just stupid? Evidently it had no sus-

icion of what lay ahead. It still sensed no danger as it
came near the edge of the trap.

One more step, and it would be caught. That would
frighten away the other elephants. They would leave the
trail and stampede through the forest, and Hal knew that
a frightened herd will sometimes cover as much as fifty
miles in a day. Hal would be left with an animal he
couldn't use – he would have to release it and start all
over again.

Then he woke up to the fact that the beast he didn't
want had stepped over the trap without knowing it was
there and was sleepily ambling on down the trail.

Now Hal had a new worry. Elephants take long steps –
suppose they all passed over without putting a foot in the
hole?

The next elephant was big and beautiful. It would do
nicely. Any zoo would be happy to have it. Hal measured
its stride with his eye. If it kept the same pace the right
forefoot should go into the hole.

The elephant stopped. A leafy branch had caught its
eye. It stepped off the trail, extended its trunk, tore off
the branch and passed the dainty morsel into its mouth
to be ground up by the great molars. Then it pushed
through the underbrush and came out on the trail again
beyond the trap.

The third knew something was wrong. It paused and
lowered its trunk and sniffed about over the leaves cover-
ing the trap. Then it cautiously stepped around the spot
and continued down the trail with a contemptuous squeal
that seemed to say:

'You'll have to be smarter than that to catch me.'

The fourth arrival was the sort of beast an animal
collector dreams about. It was a gigantic male standing

two-men high, with gleaming tusks that stretched out before him like cargo booms.

Hal refused to get excited. He was used to bad luck. He wasn't surprised when one forefoot passed safely over the trap. Another foot, safe – and another. Just one more chance.

The rear right foot went squarely into the hole. When it came out, the loop tightened around the ankle. The big tusker gave out a thunderous sort of grumble and broke into a fast shuffle.

The rope snapped taut and would certainly have broken if the end had been fastened to an immovable tree. But the log moved just enough so that the strain on the rope was not too great.

Away went the surprised giant dragging the log behind him.

He did not make rapid progress. The log was very heavy. It was two feet thick and as long as the elephant and it caught on every rock and was snagged by the bushes. Then great exertion was needed to pull it loose and drag it another two or three feet until it became snagged again.

But the shrubs in which it was repeatedly snarled acted like steel springs, always yielding a little to the pull so that the jungle-made rope was not snapped.

The big elephant shook the forest with a high-sounding scream like the shriek of a jet plane. His friends raised their voices to the same high pitch and went bulldozing through the thickets, hunting for the men who had done this thing – but the men had climbed to safety in the trees.

One pygmy who had only climbed as high as a house was snared by an angry trunk, thrown on the ground, and badly trampled. The animal then made off, assuming his victim to be dead. In such a moment of terror you could not expect even a kind-hearted elephant to give you a decent burial.

Fearing they would be caught in the same way, the other men scrambled higher. Hal was amazed at the upward reach of these animals. His one-storey home, he remembered, measured fifteen feet from ground to gable. But now he must climb at least twenty-five feet above ground to be out of reach of the snaky trunks. Then the whole herd took fright and went plunging away through the brush.

The men came down and for the next hour watched the great elephant heaving and straining to escape from the bush-bound log. Finally the animal surrendered in complete exhaustion. He stood soundless, his head hanging in defeat.

'Now what?' Hal asked Abu.

It was a long way to the village. There he had trucks with elephant cages. But how could they be brought here, since there was no road?

'We will take him to the village,' Abu said as calmly as if this were a trapped rabbit instead of a ten-ton elephant.

He called to his men. They swarmed down from the trees and gathered round the weary elephant.

The fight was not quite gone out of him. He sucked up a lot of small stones, turned his trunk in towards his mouth and then uncurled it with great force and blew the stones at his enemies. He scored several hits. Then he gave up this style of attack, for there were no more stones. And besides he was very, very tired and didn't care much what happened to him now.

The log caught in the bushes was lifted free. The men swarmed behind the elephant and along one flank and by the pricking of their spears persuaded him to turn towards the village. Then they prodded him forward, meanwhile keeping the log clear of snags.

'Why not let him loose from the log altogether?' Hal inquired.

Abu shook his head. 'He's still much strong inside,' he said. 'No log, he much danger.'

Hal sent Joro back to bring Roger and his baby. The small elephant followed Roger willingly and in a few minutes the boy and the beast had joined the party on its slow trek towards camp.

Hal sent some of his men on ahead to make ready the cage. So when the prize animal finally came out into the clearing he was greeted by the entire village, who watched his last unwilling march up an earthen ramp to the floor of the truck on which rested the enormous crate.

He was even glad to go inside to escape his tormentors. The door was dropped behind him. The rope running out under the door was left attached to the log just as an extra precaution in case the animal broke open the crate and tried to escape.

Hal looked in between the bars. Inside that cage was a good twelve thousand dollars' worth of elephant.

Hal's father would be pleased. The animal-collecting outfit of Hunt, Hunt, and Hunt had made good – thanks to the help of the smallest hunters on earth. The jinx of the Mountains of the Moon had been broken.

Hal looked up. He strained his eyes, hoping to get a glimpse of the elephants of the sky. But the snow-packed mountain peaks were entirely buried in fog. He would have liked to see if they were all there. Or had one of them, one of the biggest, come down to earth, and was it now a prisoner in this cage?

It was only a crazy fancy. But one was bound to have crazy fancies in this fantastic world of over-sized beasts, three-foot earthworms, giant flowers, giant men, and pygmies with giant courage.

He looked round to find Mumbo, towering chief of the Watussi, standing beside him. He felt like saying:

'You see you were wrong. You said we couldn't take an elephant alive. The evil spirits of the Mountains of the Moon, you said, would not permit it. Well, there's your elephant, and he's very much alive. That ought to put a kink in your favourite superstition.'

He thought of saying all this but he didn't say it. He said:

'Nice beast, isn't he?'

'Very good,' agreed Mumbo.

'He will be a great attraction in some zoo.'

Mumbo smiled gravely. 'I am sorry, my friend. He will never reach a zoo.'

Hal could hardly conceal his annoyance.

'I suppose you think he'll vanish into thin air.'

'You say it well,' Mumbo agreed. 'Vanish into thin air.' He turned his gaze upwards to the fog that concealed the mountain-tops. 'From there he came, and there he will return. I am sad to have to tell you this, my son, for I know your hopes are high. But it is better that you know.'

'Thank you,' Hal said. But he thought, Stubborn old fool. But I can't blame him. I'd get loony too if I had to live long in these crazy mountains.

14 | The leaping tent

ROGER was in trouble. His half-ton baby was almost too much for him.

'Big boy' he had named it. Big Boy seemed big to Roger, but evidently felt very small and lost without its mother.

Roger could not move ten feet without being followed at once by the squealing infant. It lumbered after him so fast that it could not stop in time and knocked him down.

Twice he tried to get to his feet and was pushed down again. Then he crawled on all fours to his tent and sneaked inside. He climbed up on to his camp-bed. It was good to lie down. He had had a big day.

He had no sooner stretched out than in between the flaps came Big Boy. Spotting Roger on the bed, he squeaked with pleasure and came to join him.

He flopped down on the edge of the bed, which promptly broke under the weight, and both elephant and boy went sprawling on the ground with the boy under the elephant.

Roger tried to call for help but the voice had been squeezed out of him. He wondered if his ribs would crack under the strain. Then the wriggling mass on top of him squirmed to one side and he was able to slip out from underneath it. He plunged out of the tent and the flaps closed behind him. He lay in the grass trying to get his breath back.

Then he sat up to see a very strange sight. His tent had come to life.

It leaped and billowed and bulged. It tore loose its guy ropes and went flouncing about like a fat woman in long skirts. Yelling pygmies jumped out of its way. Women screamed, babies cried.

It was a very noisy tent. It grunted and squealed and trumpeted like an elephant. Only Roger knew that it really *was* an elephant. With the flaps closed, Big Boy had not been able to see how to get out of the tent. So he had promptly gone wild. He went blundering about like a blind balloon.

Roger sat in the grass laughing. But when he saw the frantic ball of canvas roll over a hut, injuring a woman and a child, he realized it was no longer a laughing matter. Something must be done and he must do it, for this was his elephant.

Toto came running up with a gun. He levelled it at the galumphing tent.

'Don't do that!' Roger yelled. He called to Joro and the other safari men. 'Come on,' he shouted, and ran towards the living tent. The others guessed his purpose and joined him.

Together they laid hold of the flapping canvas on all sides, and it seemed for a minute that they had Big Boy pinned down. But the frightened animal made a mighty heave and shook off the men as if they had been flies. Big Boy trampled down another hut.

Force didn't work. Roger decided to try something else.

He ran directly in front of the charging tent.

'Look out!' yelled Hal who had just come on the scene. 'You'll get killed.'

Roger stood still and began to talk. He didn't say anything in particular. He didn't know whether he was speaking English or just making sounds – he only wanted Big Boy to hear his voice.

The oncoming tent stopped just in time to avoid running over him. It stood quivering and from it came an inquiring little squeaking sound.

Roger kept talking, quietly, soothingly. He stooped and slowly lifted the edge of the canvas.

A foot appeared – then a trembling trunk – finally a wild eye. Big Boy whimpered like the baby he was. Roger finished removing the canvas.

Now the little elephant was more determined than ever not to let Roger out of his sight. When the boy started to move away he felt a snake whip around his neck and shoulders. It was Big Boy's trunk, and when Roger attempted to break loose the grip on his throat was so tight it made him choke.

'Ow!' squealed Roger. 'Let up on me.'

Hal was laughing. 'Surely you don't mind a little affection. Must be nice to have someone think so much of you.'

'He'll kill me with kindness,' Roger complained. 'Ouch! Don't stand there laughing. Get this beast off my neck.'

'There's only one thing you can do,' Hal said. 'Give him something he loves more than he loves you.'

'What's that?'

'Food.'

'Okay – go ahead – feed him.'

Hal could not miss this chance of teasing his kid brother. He laughed.

'Feed him yourself. He's your baby.'

Just how Roger was going to feed his elephant while he was locked in its trunk, Hal did not explain. But Roger was not going to be so easily defeated.

'You think I can't do it,' he said. 'Joro, bring me some mopani leaves.'

He had noticed that elephants were fond of the leaves of this particular tree. There were many mopanis among the trees at the edge of the clearing. Joro broke off and brought a branch covered with tender green foliage. He laid it on the ground in front of Big Boy.

Roger felt the grip on his throat loosen. Big Boy uncoiled his trunk and lowered it. He passed the tip of his trunk over and through the leaves, loudly sniffing the pleasant odour.

But he didn't seem to know what to do next. He was too young to have learned how to take leaves or grass in the curl of his trunk and bring the food to his mouth. He was still used to being fed on his mother's milk. And now there was no mother.

Except Mother Roger. But that mother was even more puzzled than the baby.

Then Roger thought of the cattle. The Watussi had a large herd of them and there must be plenty of milk in the village. He called Joro.

'Get a pail from the supply truck. Go into the village and ask for a pailful of milk.'

When the milk was placed before him, Big Boy passed his trunk tip over it, sniffing as he had sniffed the leaves. Evidently he liked the smell. But it didn't seem to occur to him to suck the milk up into his trunk and then squirt it into his mouth.

15 | An elephant's table manners

ROGER was disgusted.

'I think I got myself a pretty stupid elephant.'

'Oh, I wouldn't say that,' Hal said. 'When you were his age you hadn't learned how to use a knife and fork. His trunk is his knife and fork. He just hasn't learned yet how to feed himself with it.'

'Well, I'll get that milk down his throat or die in the attempt.'

Roger picked up the pail and raised it towards the elephant's mouth. But the mouth was covered by the trunk.

'Hoist up your trunk, you nut, if you want any milk.'

When this command was not obeyed, he said to Joro, 'Joro, raise his trunk.'

Joro tried to do just that. The elephant raised his trunk, but only long enough to give Joro a good wallop with it. As the trunk whipped back it struck the pail and completely emptied the contents over Joro, Big Boy, and Roger. Dripping with milk, they were a pretty sight.

'Better give it up,' Hal suggested.

'Not on your life.' Roger sent Joro for more milk. In the meantime he quieted the excited animal by stroking its cheek.

Suddenly the elephant calf noticed the hand dripping with sweet milk and got it into his mouth.

'Look out,' Hal warned. 'He can smash your hand with one bite.'

But Roger resisted the temptation to jerk his hand out of that dangerous trap. He did not think Big Boy was going to bite him. Instead, the elephant greedily sucked the milky hand.

A great light broke over Roger. So that was the way to do it. The small elephant was used to sucking down his dinner. All Roger had to do was to keep dipping his hand into the milk and then putting it into the elephant's mouth.

But that would take all day and all night. A pailful would be needed, perhaps several, to satisfy the little beast. And Roger could tell by the feel of things that it would not be long before the powerful suction took the skin off his hand.

'No, there must be an easier way, and quicker.

'In the supply truck,' he told Mali, 'you'll find a short piece of hose. Bring it here.'

When the hose came, Roger placed one end of it in the pail of milk Joro brought. With his free hand he took the other end and slipped it into the mouth in the palm of the hand that was being sucked.

It worked like magic. The sucking drew the milk up the hose into the eager mouth and the level of the milk in the pail fell rapidly. In a few minutes the pail was empty. It was at once replaced with a full pail. That went just as fast, and so did a third pail. The calf would have taken more, but Hal said, 'that's enough for now. Cow's milk is different from what he's used to. It may give him the tummy-ache.'

Roger withdrew his hand and the hose. Hal grinned.

'I've got to hand it to you, kid. You have a way with

these beasties. If I hear of any elephant that needs a baby
sitter, I'll recommend you.'

This was high praise, coming from Hal, and Roger
puffed with pride.

But soon his baby was also puffing, and not with pride.
He was swelling up like a balloon. He began to whine
and cry, very much like a human child.

'What's the matter with him?' Roger asked his brother.

'Wind on the stomach. It's a common complaint of
elephants, especially if they have eaten something unusual.'

The calf grew fatter and his wailings louder.

'What do we do about it?'

'Well, I remember that when you were a baby and had
this trouble, mother used to burp you.'

'You can't expect *me* to remember that – how did she do it?'

'Just laid you face down over her shoulder. Then you would cough up the wind.'

Roger looked at his thousand-pound baby. Imagine putting that over your shoulder! But something must be done for the suffering beast. He scowled at Hal.

'This is no time to get funny. Tell me what to do.'

Hal shook his head. His father had always made him work out his own problems. It had made him think for himself. He must do the same for his younger brother.

'You tell me,' he said. 'I've never burped an elephant. You can think of a way to do it as well as I can. Use your own head.'

That gave Roger an idea. All right, he would use his own head. He crawled under the crying calf. He pressed his head and shoulders against the blown-up belly. He pushed up with all his might. He held this position as long as he could. He couldn't keep it up, it was too awkward and uncomfortable, and he was getting no results. That balloon needed more pressure than he could apply. Perhaps if he got more heads and shoulders ...

'Joro, Mali, Toto. Come in and help me.'

They came. Hal joined them, though he doubted that his sort of treatment would work. They all pushed and pushed and strained and sweated and accomplished nothing except to excite the little beast, which squealed more loudly and began dancing about, nearly stepping on those who were trying to help him.

The baby-burpers had to give it up. They came out, panting, wiping the sweat from their faces.

Roger was not ready to quit. There must be a way. If he could only get something stronger than heads and shoulders under that elephant. Stronger and harder. His eye wandered over the camp and the village.

Just beyond the huts was a small lake fed by streams from the glaciers and the heavy rains. On its shore lay a raft.

It was not much of a raft – only four logs firmly lashed together. But it was hard and it was strong. Also, being four feet wide, it would fit nicely beneath Big Boy's balloon.

'Could we use that?' he asked tall Chief Mumbo.

'It belongs to my son,' Mumbo said. He called the boy by name. 'Bo.'

16 | The chief's son

THE boy called Bo stepped out of the crowd. He was a
handsome lad, about Roger's own age. His skin was a
rich golden brown. His face had the fine Watussi look,
his eyes were eager and his smile was open and pleasant.
Roger liked him at once.

'Do you speak English?'

'I try. My father teach me some.'

'May we use your raft?'

'Of course. You wish to go out on the lake? I will take
you.'

'Perhaps later. I'd like to go with you. That would be
fun. But just now I want to see if your raft will help my
elephant.'

Perhaps Bo did not quite understand how a raft could
help an elephant – but he at once ordered some of the
Watussi to bring the raft. They obeyed him as promptly
and cheerfully as if he had been the chief himself. Evidently the tall folk were very fond of this boy and res-
pected him. He would be the chief when his father died
and he would make a good chief.

Six men came carrying the raft. Roger had them place
it crosswise under the elephant.

Hal could not understand what his kid brother was
up to. But he was wise enough to let the boy work things

out in his own way. It did look pretty crazy – an elephant on a raft!

Roger and his willing helper, Bo, tied a rope to each corner of the raft. While some of the men held the raft up tight against the elephant's stomach, Roger tied the four ropes together on Big Boy's back. The little elephant didn't know what to make of all this. He made angry rushes at some of the men. Anyone who came near him was apt to get poked with a sharp tusk.

Anyone except Roger, and Bo. He seemed to accept Bo as a friend. The chief's son quietened him by petting his head and trunk while the ropes were being knotted together across the animal's backbone.

Next Roger called for a tow chain. It was the same sort of chain that had been broken by the big elephant the day before. But it should be strong enough to handle this little half-tonner.

He snapped the end of the chain to the knot on the elephant's back. Then he looked up, and now for the first time Hal guessed what was on his mind. Above his head was the heavy branch of a big tree.

Roger climbed on Big Boy's back and passed the free end of the chain over the branch. Bo caught the end and drew it down until the chain was tight.

'Fantastic!' Hal muttered to himself. 'What kids will think of!'

Roger called the strongest of his safari men and had them lay hold of the loose end of the chain and pull down. This should pull the raft up hard against the baby's ballooned stomach. If they pulled hard enough the little animal would be lifted from the ground. So it would be just like a human baby across its mother's shoulder – but on a large scale.

It was a bright idea, but Roger hadn't reckoned on the weight of the baby. The men pulled and pulled until the veins stood out on their foreheads. But they couldn't raise the beast clear of the ground. All they did was to make it squeal more loudly. The shrieks of the uncomfortable little beast might have been heard a mile away.

'It's no good,' Roger said. 'Lay off.'

The men were only too happy to let go of the chain and sit down on the grass to rest. Some of the other safari men were laughing. So were some of the Watussi and the pygmies. Roger felt he had made a fool of himself.

He looked at Hal, expecting to see him laughing too. But Hal was not even smiling.

'Don't give up,' he said. 'You're on the right track. Just one little change – and you've got it.'

'What change?'

'You'll think of it.' And now he did smile.

Encouraged, Roger racked his brain. What could he do? Just one little change. What could it be? More pull on the chain – that was what he needed. But the men had done their best.

Then the answer came to him. Of course – why hadn't he thought of it before?

'Mali, back that catching truck right in here. So the tail-board will be about five feet from Big Boy.'

When the truck was in position it was the work of a moment to make fast the chain.

'Put her in four-wheel drive,' Roger said. 'Now – go ahead – easy.'

The chain began to pass, a link at a time, over the branch. The raft snugged up under Big Boy's body.

'A little more. Gently. Still a bit more.'

One of the elephant's feet left the ground. Then another and then a third. Finally all four feet were waving in the air.

Big Boy's entire weight was now pressed against the four logs. No balloon could stand this. In one mighty belch Big Boy got rig of the bothersome wind.

The little elephant felt better at once. He stopped squealing and his squeals were replaced with a low growling sound.

'He's growling at me,' Roger said. 'That's gratitude for you.'

'He's not growling,' Hal said. 'That's the nearest he can come to a purr.'

When the animal was let down and the artificial shoulder removed, he showed his appreciation so plainly that there could be no mistake. He nuzzled his head against Roger and then against Bo, all the time demonstrating his contentment and affection with a low rumbling sound deep in the throat.

Now the people were not laughing at Roger – they were laughing with him. It had been a great show. They were proud of their young guest. And their joy over his success made him happy too.

But what he appreciated most was Hal's hand on his shoulder and his brief but sufficient praise: 'Attaboy!'

17 | The giant earthworm

THE men carried the raft back to the edge of the lake, Roger and Bo helping.

'Are there any fish in this lake?' Roger asked.

'Plenty,' said Bo. 'Would you like to go fishing?'

Without waiting for an answer he ran to his father's house and brought back two lines made of papyrus fibre. At the end of each was a home-made hook fashioned from the bone of some animal. Also he brought a sort of scoop or shovel which had once been the jaw-bone of a wild pig.

'What's that for?' Roger inquired.

'To get a worm.'

Bo began digging into the soft wet ground.

'We'll need two worms,' Roger said, looking at the two bone hooks. He had forgotten for a moment what he had been told about the earthworms of the Mountains of the Moon.

Bo looked up in surprise.

'One will be enough,' he said. 'One is enough for a hundred hooks.'

He had dug about six inches deep. Suddenly the dirt moved at the bottom of the hole. Then a brown head popped out.

'Take care,' Roger said, drawing back. 'A snake!'

'Not a snake,' Bo assured him.

He grasped the thing just behind the head. He dug
until he was able to draw the whole body free. Then he
held the wriggling thing high in the air.

It was as long as a pygmy and as thick through as
Roger's wrist. The head was brown and the body a fiery
red. The ugly mouth was wide open. Otherwise the face
was a blank. Hal came up to have a look.

'It has no eyes,' Roger said. 'And no ears.'

'Just like our own earthworms,' Hal said. 'It can't hear
or smell, or taste. But it can see a little.'

'How could anything see without eyes?'

'It has tiny organs that tell it the difference between
light and dark. By day it stays under the earth. At night
it comes out. Shine a torch on it and it will promptly go
back underground.'

Down each side of the giant earthworm were two rows of bristles.

'What are they for?'

'Those are the pushers – to propel the worm through the ground while it is making its tunnel.'

'But how can it make a tunnel? Where does the dirt go?'

'Right through the worm. He swallows the dirt ahead of him, it passes through his body and is left behind him.'

'A neat trick if you can do it,' Roger admitted. 'But you said "he". How do you know it's a he?'

'I don't. I could just as well have said "she". It's really a he-she. Both sexes in the same body.'

'Another neat trick,' Roger said. 'I'm beginning to think it's rather wonderful. I always thought that worms were – well – just worms.'

'I know. Usually they're so small, they don't look like much. But when they're as big as this you can see plainly what a good job Nature has done on them.'

Roger wouldn't have minded in the least slipping an ordinary worm on to his hook, but when Bo took his knife and slashed off two chunks of the squirming monster to bait the hooks Roger actually found himself feeling sorry for the worm.

Roger and Bo boarded the raft and poled it out into the lake. There they settled down to fish. Almost at once there was a strong tug on Roger's line and he pulled in something that looked like a catfish, but far larger than any he had ever seen. Bo soon took another like it.

'Beats me,' Roger said, 'how everything here is more than life-size – except the pygmies. You Watussi are the tallest people in the world, the elephants are the biggest, the flowers and the trees are huge, even the worms.'

A thundering crash came from the hidden mountains. Roger had heard the like before, and Hal had said it was probably caused by a few million tons of ice breaking from the edge of a glacier and plunging down the cliffs. But the Watussi had a different explanation, and Bo's eyes suddenly became large and round and full of fright.

'You think we are big,' he said. 'We are small. He is the big one.'

'He?'

'Yes. The Thunder-man. He is as tall as the tallest tree. When he steps the earth shakes. When he speaks it is like the roar of a thousand lions. What you call lightning – it comes from his eyes when he is angry. If it strikes a tree the tree falls. If it strikes a village, it burns. He comes in the night. First he took only our cattle. Now he takes boys, or girls. They are here in the evening – they are gone in the morning. He will take your elephants – the big one, and the little one.'

'Not if I know it,' Roger said stoutly.

'You will not know it. Not until it is too late.'

Bo looked about nervously. On one side of the lake was the village. On the other side the forest crowded close to the shore. The shadows under the trees were very deep.

'It is getting dark now,' Bo said. 'I think we had better go in.'

They poled the raft ashore. Bo insisted that Roger take both fish, and what was left of the big worm.

'What could I do with the worm?' Roger said.

'Cook it for your supper. It is very good.'

'I don't think I'd like it. It looks too much like a snake. You wouldn't eat a snake, would you?'

'Of course. Snake meat is very tender – better than

chicken. But the worm is still better because it has no bones.'

Bones or no bones, Roger made no bones of the fact that he didn't want a worm for supper.

'I'll take the fish,' he said, 'and thank you. I'd rather you had the worm. So long. And thanks for the fishing trip. See you in the morning. Come on, Big Boy.'

The little elephant, which had been patiently waiting on shore for the return of its master, followed him closely to camp. Roger gave the two fish to the cook. During supper he told Hal what Bo had said about the 'Thunderman'.

'Craziest thing I ever heard,' Roger concluded.

'Well, yes and no,' Hal said. 'It's crazy all right, but quite natural.'

'Natural to believe in a bogey-man as tall as a tree that talks thunder and shoots lightning and steals cows and kids?'

'Lots of wild tribes all over the world believe such things,' Hal said. 'Chances are your own ancestors believed them when they lived in caves and had never seen the inside of a school and didn't know the scientific reasons for thunder and lightning and earthquakes and forest fires and floods and all that. So they thought they were the work of gods or devils. And the people in this village have been losing things, so they have good reason to be worried. Matter of fact, I'm worried too.'

'You mean you really believe this Thunder-man stuff?'

'All I know is that something or somebody is stealing cattle and kidnapping children. And I'm going to post armed guards tonight so we won't lose our elephants.'

Hal assigned two of his best men, Joro and Toto, to guard duty.

'I know you're tired,' he said. 'You've had a hard day. But all our work today will go for nothing if our elephants are stolen. I think it should be all right if you watch turn and turn about – one keep guard while the other sleeps, then change places.'

The men appreciated Hal's wish to make it easy for them.

'Don't worry about us, *bwana*,' said Joro. 'We'll be all right. And we won't let anybody take the elephants.'

Hal looked thoughtfully at Big Boy, who stood in the light of the campfire keeping an eye on Roger.

'There's one other thing,' Hal said. 'The little one – perhaps he will take it into his head to go off and rejoin the herd. He may forget about Roger – babies do forget, you know. Perhaps he will try to wander away. How will you stop him?'

'Better put him in a cage,' Toto suggested.

But when they tried to do it Big Boy objected loudly. He kicked and bucked and squealed. He broke away, ran to Roger and stood close to him, running the tip of his trunk over the boy's bush jacket. Evidently he found comfort in the smell of it, because it belonged to his master.

'We could take him into the tent with us,' Roger said.

'And have him smash your bed again and carry off the tent the way he did this afternoon? No thanks.'

He watched the little elephant sniffing at Roger's jacket.

'That's it,' Hal said. 'Let's try it.'

'Try what?'

'Take off your jacket. Hang it on that branch. Now, while he's still interested in the jacket, sneak into the tent.'

Roger disappeared into the tent. Big Boy saw him go and whimpered once, but knowing his master was near, he was quite satisfied to stand by the jacket, the smell of which had come to mean the smell of a good friend.

The boys turned in. In ten seconds they were asleep. All night they slept as hard as they had worked all day. It would have taken nothing less than an explosion to waken them.

18 | Kidnapped

T H E explosion came at dawn.

It was an explosion of voices – the screams of women, the crying of children, the angry shouts of men.

Roger was out of his bed and out of the tent all in one movement. The bush jacket still hung on the branch. Big Boy was gone.

Hal was out now, and both boys raced to the cage.

It was empty.

The village was in an uproar. The tall folk and the short folk ran in all directions like frightened ants.

Chief Mumbo came striding over to the boys as they stood looking into the vacant cage.

'The elephants are gone,' Hal said.

It didn't seem to matter to Chief Mumbo in the least. He had something far more important on his mind.

'My son,' he said. 'Have you seen my son?' His voice, usually so deep and dignified, rose to a cry. 'He has taken my son!'

Others came running to report that two of the best cattle were missing. Cattle were almost as precious as children to the Watussi. But the wailing and weeping of the villagers was not for the theft of their cattle but for the loss of Bo, beloved son of their chief.

What added to the mystery was that the chief lived in a real house, no mere hut, with a lock on the door, the only lock in the village.

'Wasn't your door locked?' Hal asked.

'Of course.'

'Then how could anybody get in?'

'You don't understand,' Mumbo said. 'He is an evil spirit, the Thunder-man. Locks are nothing to him.'

'How about the two guards we posted last night?' wondered Roger. 'Have they been kidnapped too?'

Hal questioned the safari men. Had they seen Joro and Toto? They had not.

A search was made through the bushes near the big cage and the tree of the bush jacket. In one place the bushes were beaten and broken as if there had been a fight at that point.

The hunt was carried farther back into the woods. Hal kept calling:

'Joro! Toto!'

No answer. Hal's heart sank. Had he lost two of his best men? Then he heard Roger shout:

'Here they are!'

Hal ran to see. In a hollow behind a great rock lay the two men. They were bound hand and foot and their mouths were gagged. They looked as if they had been very roughly treated, but they were alive. The boys pulled out the gags and cut the ropes.

'What happened?' Hal asked.

Joro hung his head. 'We have very much shame. Toto was taking his turn to sleep. I was watching. I did not close my eyes – but I was very tired. I heard no one coming. Suddenly a hand – over my mouth. I tried to call out. They gagged me with that cloth. They gagged Toto before he could awake. We fought – but they tied our hands and feet and dumped us into this hole'.

'Were there many of them?'

'Many.'

'What kind of men?'

'We could not see. But I know that they were not black. And they were not white.'

'You're talking nonsense,' Hal said. 'How could you tell their colour when you couldn't see them?'

'By the smell. They did not smell of sun and earth like the black man. Nor of tobacco like the white man. They smelled of tea and mint and they had the smell of the ships with sail that come to Mombasa from the north.'

'Arabs!' guessed Hal. 'But what could Arabs be doing in these mountains?'

Chief Mumbo did not understand this talk about Arabs.

'They were evil spirits,' he said. 'And their great spirit is the Thunder-man. Was he here?'

'I know nothing about your Thunder-man,' Joro said.

'His head is in the stars. When he speaks it is thunder and his eyes make lightning.'

'There was no thunder and no lightning.'

Mumbo nodded. 'He stilled his voice and made dark his eyes so he would not wake us. But was there not one strong as an ox and tall as a tree?'

'How tall, I could not tell in the dark. But strong as an ox – yes. At first many men laid hold of me. I am strong and I shook them off. Then two great hands closed upon me. They crushed me. They made me weak like water. Never have I felt hands so strong.'

'Yes, yes!' said Mumbo in great excitement. 'That was the Thunder-man. He took my son. We will never get him back. No man alive can fight the Thunder-man.'

'We can fight him and we will,' Hal said. 'We'll get your son back if it is humanly possible. Sorry, chief, I don't go for your spook stories. If there was anybody here last night bigger and better than our own men, I'll eat my hat.'

Roger was studying the ground.

'Get ready to eat your hat,' he said. 'Look at these footprints.'

Most of the prints in the mud were made by bare feet and their size was not unusual. But there were also deep heavy impressions made by huge boots.

Hal suddenly felt much smaller than a moment ago. A thin cool line of fear ran up his backbone. He was sure that his antagonist was no spook. But it was just as clear that he was no ordinary man. He must be a giant to wear such boots. He must be very heavy to make such deep marks in the mud. But his heaviness could not be mere fat – it was muscle, terrific muscle, and Joro had felt the power of it.

But that was not all. This giant had more than muscle. He had skill – the skill to creep up silently upon the camp, gag and tie two guards, pick a lock and remove a boy from the chief's house without allowing him to make a sound, steal cattle, and, most difficult of all, drive off two lumbering elephants without exciting them to a single squeal or rumble.

But Hal would not let anyone see his uneasiness. He said:

'The fellow's big boot-prints will just make it easier for

us to track him. Time out for breakfast – then we hit the trail.'

Twenty minutes later they were on their way, following the big boot-prints and the even larger footprints of the two elephants. Joro and Toto insisted on coming along in spite of their hard night. Joro was Hal's chief tracker, and with his help he was sure they could track the gang to its lair. Some of the men of the village wanted to go, but Chief Mumbo forbade it.

'Would you bring destruction on us all?' he said. 'You will do that if you make the Thunder-man angry. With one hand he could crush this village. I too would like to go after Bo, for I am his father. But I am also chief and must think of the welfare of all of you.'

At first the tracking was very easy. Even if there had been no human footprints it would have been a simple matter to follow the deep, broad holes made by the two elephants.

Each forefoot of the big elephant made a round print two feet in diameter and about three inches deep. The print of each hind foot was not round, but oval, leaving a depression that looked like a big platter, three feet long and two wide.

No other animal in all the world could leave so big and so plain a record of his passing.

'This is almost too easy,' Roger laughed. 'Those Arabs can't be so smart after all. We're bound to come up with them soon and then we'll give them what's what.'

Hal was studying the human prints. He asked Joro:

'How many men do you think there were?'

'Perhaps twelve, perhaps fifteen.'

'And we have thirty,' Roger said happily. 'It will be no job at all to rub them out.'

'But they may have more men at their camp,' Hal reminded him. 'And they must have known they were leaving a plain trail. It won't stay so plain, nor so safe. Somewhere, they'll try to trick us. Keep your eyes peeled.'

A forest of wild flowers rose high over their heads. The stems of the flowers were as big as tree trunks. Lobelias stood like gigantic candles twenty feet tall. The blooms at their tops were like flames.

The scene changed, and they were in a forest of bamboo. Far above, the ceiling of long pointed leaves was a delicate green against the dark sky. The constant mist made the leaves wet and from them fell drops of water like pearls to the always wet earth. The thick bamboo trunks were as straight as the columns in a cathedral.

'Must take them a long time to grow so big,' Roger said.

'You'd be surprised,' Hal said. 'You see, it's never dry here for one minute. They grow like mad. A hundred feet in two months. I'm not kidding.' He grinned at the look of astonishment on Roger's face. 'Just think,' he went on, 'at home we have to wait twenty to fifty years for a tree to grow a hundred feet high, depending on what sort of tree it is. Of course, bamboos grow fast anywhere, but faster here than anywhere else.'

'So all these big trees are only two months old? I can't believe it.'

'It's true.'

'Will they keep on going higher?'

'No – a hundred feet is about the limit.'

'Then what happens?'

'They bloom – just once. Then they die. The seeds that the flowers have dropped take root and make new trees.

There's one now – just starting.'

The bamboo shoot, as thick as Roger's leg, stood a foot high.

'It wasn't there yesterday,' Hal said. 'It popped up overnight.'

'How do you know?'

'Scientific expeditions have been through here. They took measurements. It's all in the botany books – you can look it up for yourself. A shoot will grow almost two feet a day for the first few weeks. It slows down later. But a lot of them never get a chance to grow.'

'Why not?'

'They're eaten by animals. Bamboo shoots are tender and sweet.'

'I know. We've had them in Chinese restaurants.'

'Right. The Watussi and the pygmies love them. And they're the favourite food of gorillas. Look – the gorillas have been here.'

The footprints were plain. They had been made by bare feet, but certainly not the feet of any man. Compared with these huge impressions, the prints left by Hal's safari men looked as if they had been made by children.

Otherwise they looked quite human. It was easy to see the marks left by the five toes.

'But why are the prints so deep?'

'Because the gorilla is so heavy. A big male gorilla can weigh 700 pounds – four times the weight of the average man.'

'If they were right here why didn't they chew up that bamboo shoot?'

'They may have been here yesterday before it was out of the ground. Come on, pal – we're being left behind.

If there are any of these hairy gentlemen around I don't care to meet them alone.'

'What do you mean, alone? You have me.'

Hal laughed. 'Lot of help you'd be! A gorilla could knock you out with one little love pat.' He looked around. 'They're probably watching us right now.'

'Well, we don't need to worry,' Roger said comfortably. 'If any of the big brutes had wanted to make trouble he would have attacked our men.'

'Attack a gang of thirty men? Not likely. But two little babes in the woods like us – we'd be easy pickings.'

'If they're like most animals they won't bother us unless we bother them.'

'You got that out of story-books,' Hal said. 'And it's true. All the same, it's nonsense. Because you never know what is going to bother them.'

The boys hurried to overtake the others, who had disappeared down the trail. It was raining in earnest now and the black clouds made the forest dark and lonely. There were deep, low sounds all about which made the boys look now here and now there, expecting to see a gorilla pop out from behind any tree.

'There's a gorilla's nest,' Hal said.

It was a very rough structure made of branches and twigs so interlaced that they made a springy mattress raised about two feet from the ground.

'I thought they lived in trees.'

'They can climb trees – but they don't want to. They're so heavy, branches might break under them. The biggest of them never leave the ground.'

The muttering sounds of the forest increased and seemed to draw closer. Roger put on a brave front. No 'monkey' was going to make a monkey out of him. He

pushed ahead and led the way. He was getting hungry.
It was not long after breakfast but, like most boys, he had
a hollow leg. In the gloom, he made out another bamboo
shoot. If a gorilla could eat it, so could he. He slashed it
off with his bush knife.

19 | The annoyed gorilla

THE darkness was pierced by a scream that made the skin crawl on Roger's back. Within five feet of him was a blackness that he had thought to be a shadow. Now he saw it was an enormous gorilla as tall as a Watussi, and as broad as three or four of them, and all black except for gleaming white teeth. His deep-sunken eyes were black, his nostrils were like black rubber and his beard like a black brush.

He thrust out a black arm and grabbed the shoot from Roger's hand. He flung it into the bushes where it was received by squeaking gorilla babies. Then he began hammering on his own huge chest, making a deep booming sound. This wasn't enough for him, and he continued to scream.

It was a lesson Roger would never forget. You couldn't tell what would bother an animal – and before you found out you might be dead. This big beast had gone into a rage merely because someone was stealing his family's lunch.

With his heart thumping like an outboard motor, Roger started to back away. He couldn't fight this thing. Neither he nor Hal carried a gun. They had only their bush knives, which would be about as useful as toothpicks against this monster.

Roger backed into Hal, who had not moved.

'Hold your ground,' Hal said. 'Don't give an inch. If he knows you're afraid he'll twist your head off.'

Hal edged forward until he stood beside Roger. The gorilla continued to scream and to pound his chest. His enormous arms were covered with hair eight inches long. His hands were as big as hams.

'Let's talk back in his own language,' Hal said.

He began beating on his own chest. He bared his teeth, twisted his usually pleasant face until it was almost as ugly as the gorilla's, and screamed at the top of his lungs. Roger followed his example.

The bamboo forest rang with the combined racket of two lusty-throated humans and the beating and bellowing of the great ape. A chorus of other gorilla voices and drums sounded on all sides, and the birds above joined in the general excitement.

Some of the safari men came running back to learn what had happened to their young masters. They stopped and stared at the strange spectacle – the hairy Hercules trying to scare two boys, while the boys, refusing to be scared, made most awful faces, whacked their own ribs, yelled to high heaven, and seemed ready to tussle with a monster that was twice as big as both of them put together.

Before the men could collect their wits they saw that the boys had already won the contest. The gorilla stepped back a few inches. The boys at once stepped forward. They brandished their arms as if about to tear the big fellow limb from limb.

The gorilla stopped his noise. His expression changed completely. Now there was fear in those deep eyes.

He turned to one side, dropped his hands to the ground, and, doubling his fists so he could walk on the knuckles as is the way of gorillas, shuffled off on all fours into the bush. He left a trail of footprints and knuckleprints and two boys, who only now began to realize that they had been badly frightened.

'My legs are like spaghetti,' Roger complained.

Hal grinned. 'You probably need some nourishment. Do have some bamboo shoots.'

'I'd starve first,' Roger said, looking round to see if any black eyes were watching. 'So far as I'm concerned, from now on bamboo shoots are strictly for the apes.'

The boys rejoined the party. It was with a great feeling of relief that they came out of the dark shades of the bamboo forest on to an open savannah.

Ahead lay a lake – beautiful even in the pouring rain. Hal identified it on his map as Green Lake.

That was another odd thing about this mountain slope. It was a series of balconies, and on each balcony was a lake. Explorers had named them Green Lake, Black Lake, White Lake, and Grey Lake. Each was kept full by the daily rains and streams coming down from the glaciers. From every balcony waterfalls tumbled to the lower level. And across Green Lake beside the waterfalls towered posies that at home you would wear in your buttonhole and here stood twenty, thirty, forty feet high.

Joro was worrying.

'The rain is washing out the footprints,' he said. 'If it keeps up like this we're going to lose the trail.'

Suddenly Joro stopped. On the rim of a giant flower directly in front of his nose was one of the most frightful-looking creatures of the Mountains of the Moon. It was a chameleon with a fishy-looking skin, pop-eyes, and three horns sprouting from its ugly forehead.

'It's a bad sign,' Joro said. 'When you see one of these

things, you must turn back. We will only have bad luck if we go on.'

Hal, who never had much patience with native superstitions, said:

'We'll go on just the same. We're not going to be stopped by one silly little animal.'

The other men had halted now and were staring with horror at the evil-looking reptile. Like Joro, they were all in favour of going back to camp.

'Listen, men,' Hal said. 'You are brave. You face the greatest of beasts without fear. You wrestle with the elephant and the rhino and the lion. Don't tell me you are afraid of a little animal that can neither sting nor bite.'

He held his finger close to the creature's mouth. The men stared in frightened silence. The chameleon did not move. A fly lit on Hal's finger. Immediately a long tongue like that of a snake darted out, took the fly, and carried it into the chameleon's mouth.

'Like an ant-eater,' Hal said to Roger. 'Its tongue is very long and very sticky and any insect it touches just has no chance.'

The eyes of the weird creature revolved on pivots. It could look at two different objects at the same time. One eye was fixed on Roger and the other on Hal. The eyes stood far out, and it was very odd indeed when one stared up and the other one down. This alone would be enough to make the Africans regard the creature with super-stitious awe.

Another reason for thinking it must be bewitched was its ability to change colour. Just now it lay on a blue part of the flower and its skin was blue. Hal picked it up and placed it on the part of the flower which was orange. The colour of the skin turned to orange.

'You see,' Joro said. 'It has magic.'

'I'll show you some more magic,' Hal said. He poked the little creature several times with his finger-nail. It swelled up like a balloon. The men shrank back mutter-ing.

'That's its way of trying to scare anybody who annoys it,' Hal said. 'It blows itself up with air – just like certain fish. The puffer fish, the globe-fish, the porcupine fish, they can all swell up to make themselves look bigger than they really are and frighten their enemies. But surely you won't let this little brat frighten you! How about Bo – the chief's son – don't you care what happens to him? And our elephants – are you going to stand by and let them take our elephants?'

'It is bad luck,' Joro repeated. 'We go back to camp.'

'Then we'll have to go on without you,' Hal said.

He passed the chameleon and struck out down the trail. Roger caught up with him.

They had not gone half a mile before Joro came
running up beside them.

'You will not come back?' he said.

'No,' Hal answered. 'But you don't need to come.'

'I will go with you.'

'But how about your bad luck?'

'If there is bad luck, we will have it together.'

Hal was deeply moved by the black man's loyalty. He
knew this was no small thing that Joro had done – daring
to break a taboo hundreds of years old. To him, passing
that chameleon was as serious a matter as it would be for
Hal to throw himself in front of a moving train.

But Joro was not to be the only one. In a few moments
Toto, the gunbearer, arrived, panting. When Hal looked
at him in surprise he said:

'I thought you might need this.' He patted the big
rifle.

'All right,' Hal said, 'I'll take it, and you go back.'

Toto clung to the rifle. 'No, no – it is for me to carry.'

After all, he was very proud of his job. The gunbearer
on an African safari is an important person. He must keep
the weapon in good condition and be ready to put it into
the hands of his master at a second's notice. Toto had
never failed, and Hal was sure he never would.

He was also sure of the rest of his men and was not
surprised when they came up, one by one, until the number was complete.

20 | The blackbirders

THE rain was falling heavily, and the cloud that it came from had settled down around the travellers so that they could hardly see ten feet ahead.

But they could still make out the elephants' tracks, the large boot-prints, and the prints of bare feet. Among these were smaller prints probably made by the feet of the chief's son.

'Poor little Bo!' Hal said. 'Such a handsome lad. They tell me all the boys and girls that have been taken were the handsome ones. Why should the kidnappers care whether they were good-looking or not?'

'I think I know,' Joro said. 'But I am not sure.'

'What do you think you know?'

'The kidnap men – they are slavers. They steal boys and girls and then sell them. They want only beautiful ones because they can sell them for much money.'

Roger perked up his ears.

'You really mean – sell them?'

'Yes, *bwana.*'

'But that isn't allowed. I mean – there are laws. All that old slave trade, it was stopped about a hundred years ago.'

'Joro may be right,' Hal said. 'Of course, the big slave trade across the Atlantic was stopped long ago. But the little slave trade still goes on through Africa's back

door – over here on the Indian Ocean side. Of cours
there are laws against it. Heavy fines if the slavers ge
caught. But they get away with it when no one is looking
There was a long story about it in the Nairobi papers onl
two weeks ago.'

'But how do they do it? Where will they take Bo, an
these other kids?'

'Probably to the Arabian peninsula. Up there the
pay a lot for slaves.' He looked at Roger with a calculat
ing eye. 'I'd say you might bring a cool thousand dollars
More if you were handsome.'

'Thanks – I'm not for sale. It all sounds like hooey t
me. How could those desert rats pay such prices fo
slaves?'

'Desert rats, indeed! There are plenty of millionaire
in the Arab countries. The sheiks own oil wells, and th
more oil wells they have the more they can afford to pa
for slaves. They take pride in having as many as possible
Instead of counting a man's wealth in the number c
Cadillacs he owns, people count in slaves – "he's only
ten-slave sheik", or "he's a thousand-slave sheik". It i
estimated that there are half a million slaves in th
Arabian peninsula and the number is increasing by abou
ten thousand a year. It's good business for the dhows.'

'What are dhows?'

'Joro can tell you – he lives down on the coast nea
Mombasa.'

'The dhows,' Joro explained, 'are Arab ships wit
sails but no engines. They come down to our coast wit
a load of carpets and shawls, dried shark, flamingo sal
dates, and oil in tall jars. They take back cargoes o
timber, charcoal, coffee, some animals – and slaves. Mos
of these dhows come between December and April. The

we send our young people away into the forest so they will not be taken. When the south-west monsoon begins to blow the dhows sail away and we bring home our young people. But we never get all of them back. The smugglers even go far into the forest to steal them. It's big business.'

'So big,' Hal said, 'that the United Nations has appointed a committee to investigate it. They find it a hard nut to crack. It will take years to stop it – but they hope to put an end to it by 1980. Joro, have you actually seen these dhows loading slaves?'

'I have seen. They creep into small bays near my home at night. I hide in the bushes and watch. I see the blackbirders . . .'

'What are blackbirders?' Roger asked.

'Just another name for the slave-runners,' Hal put in.

'I see the blackbirders,' Joro went on, 'come out of the forest driving the ones they have taken. The boys and the girls, they have chains on their ankles, and they are very tired and some of them are crying. If they refuse to do as the blackbirders say they are whipped. Also there are a few elephants, gazelles, and cattle – the sheiks of Araby pay good money for them. The blackbirders drive all on board, tie the animals on deck, and put the young people down in the hold, which has no light and no air and smells very bad.'

'Have you been on one of these dhows?'

'Many times. I go to sell coffee from my farm. Last year there was no coffee, I was very poor, and I took a job on a dhow. We sailed at midnight. The dhow goes fast on the wind because its hull is smeared with fish oil to make it slip easily through the water. Still the voyage took many days. Then we landed on a desert coast. Many people had come on camels and in cars to buy slaves. The boys and girls of Africa were driven out of the ship and up on to what they called the *dakkat al abeeb*, the slave platforms, where everybody could see them. The children were very sad. The chains had made sores on their ankles. They were hungry, and the sun was very hot. But the slavers had no pity. There was a man who did the selling.'

'An auctioneer?' Hal suggested.

'Yes. He brought out a boy – about as old as Bo. He said, "How much for this boy?" He made him walk up and down. He was sold to the one who would give most. He was thrown on a camel like a sack of coffee and he was taken away. All the children – they were all sold and taken away. The animals too. The dhow sailed back to Africa to get more. I went back to my farm. I do not like the dhows. I will never go on another dhow.'

'I should think,' Roger said, 'the United Nations could clear this thing up in no time if they'd just go on board these dhows with some soldiers and set the kids free.'

'They tried,' Hal said. 'They voted on it – to give the U.N. the right to search and seize slave ships. Egypt, Sudan, Saudi Arabia, and Yemen blocked the plan. Russia also voted no.'

'It all sounds too wild,' Roger said. 'You mean to tell me, if I walked into one of these slave markets I could buy a slave?'

'Of course. And I heard of an Englishman who did it. He was Viscount Maugham, a member of the House of Lords which refused to believe that slavery still existed. He wanted to show them that it did. On a motor trip through the Sahara he stopped near Timbuctoo and bought a twenty-year-old slave named Ibrahim for £36.

He reported this to the House of Lords. He said, "Of course, I gave him his freedom. I only wanted to prove that slavery still flourishes."'

'Yeah, but when? I'll bet that was a couple of hundred years ago.'

'It was in August 1960. And just a few weeks ago something stranger than that happened. A lot of British farmers got a circular from a white man in Southern Rhodesia offering to sell them black men for £145 down and £5 a month for two years. I doubt if he made any sales. But it just shows what goes on. And I'll bet this fellow with the big boots who took Bo is a blackbirder.'

'I smelt him,' Joro said. 'He had the smell of the dhows.'

'Well I hope you smell him again, and soon,' Roger said. 'We'd better speed up if we're going to get Bo before he's shipped away in some stinking dhow.'

They came to the edge of the lake. Here the tracks ended. Even the expert tracker, Joro, was puzzled.

'They were very clever,' he said. 'There is no way to tell where they went from here. We know that they went into the water – but then what? They may have turned left and gone off through the shallow water near the shore. They may have turned right and followed that shore. They could have swum across the lake – but in what direction?'

'Could the elephants swim?' Roger asked.

'They swim very well,' Hal said. 'But they often prefer to walk. If the water isn't too deep, they walk along the bottom even if their heads have to be under water.'

'Then how do they breathe?'

'By putting the end of their trunk up above the surface, like a periscope.'

'But they must leave tracks in the lake bottom,' Roger said.

Joro was peering into the water. If there were any tracks, he would surely see them. He waded into the shallows, still looking. He could see even less now, because his wading raised a light, powdery mud that turned the water brown. His feet sank up to the ankles in the squishy mud.

He came back to shore. The sediment he had stirred up slowly settled and the water cleared. His footprints had filled again. There was no sign whatever of his tracks.

The same thing must have happened to the tracks of the elephants and the blackbirders. The mud pudding had flowed into them and left a lake bottom as smooth as if it had never been disturbed.

'But they must have come out of the lake somewhere,' Hal said. 'We can just follow the lake shore all the way round until we get to the place where the footprints come out.'

Joro did not seem so sure that this would work, but there was nothing else to do. They set out to the left along the shore, Joro in the lead, watching carefully for tracks. The cold rain kept pouring down and the men were distinctly uncomfortable and almost rebellious.

At the west end of the lake the walking grew worse. The ground was no longer solid, but only a soft muck of deep, black mud into which the men sank up to their knees. Consulting his map, Hal found that this was the famous Beego Bog – explorers had written about its terrors. It was like a thick soup made of equal parts of soil and water. It sucked a man's foot down and down so that it was difficult to pull it out and take another step.

You couldn't call it a quicksand because there was no

sand. You might call it a quickmud. Joro suddenly went in up to his waist. The other men had to haul him out. Then the mist cleared a little and Roger cried:

'Look! Our elephants!'

Two elephants could be dimly seen, one large, one not so large.

Roger stumbled ahead so eagerly that he tripped on a mossy tussock and went head first into the mud bath. The pudding closed over him and there was no Roger.

Hal and Toto groped about in the mud and at last found his arms and pulled him out. He was a sad-looking affair, plastered with mud from head to foot, but he wiped the mushy stuff out of his eyes and struggled on, calling to his little elephant:

'Big Boy! Am I glad to see you!'

Then he saw that it was not Big Boy, and the larger elephant also was a stranger. And they were in trouble. The smaller one, a young bull, was stuck in the mud hole, and the larger, apparently its mother, was trying to get it out.

The men, so deep in mud that they were hardly able to move, could do nothing but watch.

21 | The bull in the bog

THE young bull squealed with fright. He was steadily sinking. Every time he struggled he sank a little deeper.

His mother wrapped her trunk around his and tried to lift him. It didn't work. She got her tusks under his flank and heaved, but he did not budge.

She looked towards the men and trumpeted for help. But they could not help. Then she took the last desperate measure, though it might cost her her own life.

She plunged her head under the surface and ran it beneath the body of the young bull so that his weight came on the back of her neck. Then she hoisted with all her gigantic strength.

Up came the young bull, his feet making loud sucking noises as they were pulled free of the mud. He struggled over grass lumps and through holes until he got to firm ground. There he stood, breathing hard, and looking back.

He could not see his mother. Her mighty effort to lift him out of the quickmud had made her sink so deep that she could not pull free. Her body was now completely submerged except for the tip of her trunk, which still rose a few inches above the surface, drawing in air. A minute later this also disappeared.

Greater love than this, no mother, animal or human, ever had for her child. The men stood looking with open

mouths, and tears rolled down some of the black faces.
Africans do not weep easily.

Then they woke up to the fact that they would join the
big elephant in a watery grave if they did not get out of
this infernal bog. Wallowing and splashing through the
liquid mud, they stumbled up finally on to solid ground
beside the young bull.

The youngster trembled with cold and kept calling for
his mother. He paid no attention to the men. He was
larger and older than Big Boy, but he had probably never
seen humans before and had no reason to be afraid of
them. So when Roger walked up to him and started
wiping away the mud from his eyes and round his mouth
he took it as a matter of course. When Roger moved away
he did as all young elephants are inclined to do when
deprived of their mothers. He followed the new friend.

The men had had enough. Hal could not ask them to do more – not today. Besides, as Joro pointed out, the rain must by this time have wiped out all tracks. So they made the long dreary march back to camp.

Roger was really hungry now, but as they passed through the bamboo forest under the eyes of muttering gorillas, he had no appetite whatever for bamboo shoots. Chief Mumbo ran to meet the mud-plastered hunters as they entered the village.

'Did you find my son?'

Hal sadly shook his head.

The chief raised his grief-stricken eyes to the unseen mountains and murmured:

'It is the will of the Thunder-man. I shall never see my son again.'

'Don't give up yet,' Hal said. 'We haven't quit trying. By the way, have you notified the Congo police?'

'We sent a messenger down to Mutwanga. I think it will do no good. The Congo is a country of much trouble – the police are too busy to hunt for one small boy.' Shaking his head mournfully he returned to his house.

Hal and Roger and all their muddy men plunged into the lake. The young bull followed and Roger sent to the supply wagon for a stiff brush with which he gave the hide a thorough scrubbing, much to the delight of the elephant who showed his pleasure with a deep rumbling purr. He sucked up water in his trunk and flung it over himself and everyone else.

When dinner was served he proved as hungry as any of his new friends. He turned up his six-foot nose at cow's milk, for he was quite old enough to eat solid food, and put away several hundred pounds of mopani brush.

'What do we do tonight?' Roger wondered. 'The blackbirders would steal him, just as they took Big Boy.'

'He ought to be safe in a cage,' Hal suggested.

The young bull would not enter a cage until Roger went in first – then he followed quite willingly. Roger slipped out again and locked the door.

The bull complained loudly and thrust his trunk out between the slats. Roger gently stroked the trunk until the animal accepted his lot and settled down.

Then Roger made the door doubly secure with another padlock.

'I'd like to see them try to open that,' he said.

'But we'll take no chances,' said Hal. 'We'll post guards.'

Since the safari men were dog-tired, Chief Mumbo supplied the guards. Two tough Watussi armed with spears took their place before the cage door.

The cry made by an excited elephant is like nothing else on earth.

You may call it a scream, but that's only the half of it. You may call it a shriek. But it is much more than that. It is not like the roar of a lion or the bellow of a buffalo or the snort of a rhino.

Put all these together and you still don't have it. It begins deep down in the cavernous inside of the world's largest land animal, and goes up and up until it seems it must split your head open. It is a combination of deep thunder, the rip of a circular saw through a knot, the deafening din of an iron foundry and the rising screech of a fire siren or air-raid siren. It chills your spine and makes the skin creep on the ends of your fingers.

However you describe it, it is bound to wake the

soundest sleeper. And when it came just before dawn it
ripped Roger's eyes open and left him tingling as if he
had touched a high-tension wire.

For a moment he lay frozen. Then he wrenched himself out of bed and ran out to see what had happened to
his young bull elephant.

Near the cage door he stumbled over something and
fell. Under him was the still-warm body of one of the
guards. He felt for the pulse. The man was dead. A few
feet away his groping hands found the other guard, also
dead.

Hal was with him now. Men began to come out of the
tents of the camp and the huts of the village. The elephant
was still tearing the night apart with all the power of his
steam-boiler lungs.

The truck on which the cage rested squeaked and
groaned as the wildly charging animal crashed against
one side and then the other of his cage.

'What's the matter with him?' Hal wondered.

'Probably frightened by the blackbirders.'

Roger felt for the locks. One of them had been picked
open. The other had held fast.

Roger ran back to the tent and got the key. Then he
proceeded to unlock the cage door.

'What's the idea?' Hal asked.

'He's had a bad scare,' Roger said. 'I'm going to go in
there and quiet him down.'

'He'll kill you.'

'No he won't. He knows me.'

He slipped inside the cage.

'Whoa, boy. There, there. It's all right.'

He was surprised to find that his words had no effect.
Perhaps the elephant was making too much noise to be

able to hear him. The rampaging beast knocked him over.
He got unsteadily to his feet just in time to be jammed
hard against the cage wall. A little more pressure and his
ribs would have cracked under the strain.

He felt for the trunk. If he could stroke that, he might
quiet the frenzied beast.

He found an ear, and then a tusk. Then his hand was
where the trunk should be, but there was no trunk.
Instead, a sticky liquid that smelled like blood was spat-
tering his hand.

Reaching a little higher, he touched raw, wet flesh.
This then was what was left of the trunk.

In a flash he understood. The blackbirders, after killing the two guards, had tried to steal the elephant. But
they had been unable to undo one of the locks. The
young bull, seeking a friend, had put his trunk out between the slats just as he had done the night before. The
blackbirders, furious because they could not steal the
animal and sell it to some wealthy sheik, had ruined it
so it would be of no use to anyone. No zoo would want
a trunkless elephant.

They doubtless knew that no other part of the animal
is so sensitive as the trunk. Cutting it off would mean
terrible pain, and the animal would go wild and perhaps
kill its keepers.

Roger leaped for the door. He must get out fast before
he was crushed against the slats or trampled underfoot.

He got out fast – thanks to a pair of tusks that scooped
him out of the door and flung him fifteen feet to fetch
up head first against a big rock. He fell limp and bloody
to the ground.

Hal pulled him out of the way as the insane bull rushed
from the cage and began laying about him at everything

and everybody within reach.

Men, women, and children scattered like leaves before a hurricane. Many were knocked down and badly hurt.

Mad with pain, the bull attacked the huts, tearing open the papyrus walls with his tusks, tossing the thatch of the roofs high in the air, and trampling upon anyone who happened to be inside.

Suddenly there was the crash of a heavy gun and the bull dropped in his tracks.

In the faint beginning of dawn Roger saw the gun in Hal's hands. At that moment he bitterly hated his brother.

'What did you do that for?'

'What else was there to do?'

'If you'd given me a few more minutes,' Roger said, 'I could have quieted him.'

'A few more minutes, and a lot of people would have been killed. He was crazy with pain. It was better to end his suffering.'

'We have drugs,' Roger objected. 'We could have stopped the pain – and bandaged up the trunk. In a few weeks he'd have been as good as new.'

'Listen, kid,' Hal said patiently, 'I know how you feel. But it's better this way. You know well enough that he'd never grow a new trunk. And the stump would never stop hurting, even if he lived to be a hundred. That's because it's just one solid mass of nerves. He'd be a killer all the rest of his life. And how do you suppose he'd feed himself without a trunk? How would he drink? He couldn't live in the wilds – and he couldn't live in a zoo, because no zoo would take him. Think it over.'

The villagers were already attacking the body with knives, rejoicing in the opportunity to stuff themselves with the tender meat. It made Roger sick to watch them. The young bull had been his friend. Now he was only meat.

Roger had lost him, and he had lost Big Boy. Everything had gone wrong. All the big elephants they had tackled – they hadn't been able to take one. The expedition was a failure. He could almost believe there was some evil spell over these crazy mountains. It had been just one bitter disappointment after another, and now his brother had made it more than bitter.

He looked angrily at Hal. But when he saw his brother's unhappy face, he suddenly realized that Hal must be just as sad about this whole business as he was. Perhaps sadder, because Hal was responsible for the success of the project. But Hal had not complained.

Roger regretted his angry remarks. He put his hand on Hal's arm.

'Sorry,' he said.

Hal grinned. 'That's okay. Keep your chin up. We may come out on top yet.'

22 | Big Boy escapes

OVER a hearty breakfast of antelope steak, cornmea
pancakes, and coffee, they discussed the events of th
night with Joro.

'I've never known anything quite so cruel,' Hal sai
'Cutting off that young beast's trunk! Just in spite. The
couldn't steal him, so they spoiled him. They knew he'
go mad, and they hoped he'd kill the lot of us. Wha
devils they must be! You know, I was keen to ge
elephants. Well, I still am, but I'd like even better to ge
hold of that gang of cut-throats. They must have mad
plenty of tracks last night. Do you think we could follo
them?'

Joro shook his head. 'It would be as it was yesterda
They would lead us to water and there we would lo
them.'

'If we only knew where to look!' Hal said. 'But th
mountain region is about as big as all England.'

'And the going isn't easy,' Roger added. 'No nic
paved roads – nothing but bogs and lakes and jungl
and cliffs and glaciers.'

'Anyhow,' Hal said wearily, 'we've got to keep try
ing.' There was not too much hope in his voice. 'Te
the men to be ready to start in an hour.'

Roger suddenly went up from his camp stool like

ocket, upsetting the folding table and what was left of he breakfast.

'Look!' he cried. 'It's Big Boy.'

The baby elephant was just emerging from the forest. He stopped and looked about. Then he saw Roger. He trumpeted loudly and came as fast as his stubby legs would carry him.

Roger ran to meet him. They collided so hard that Roger was nearly knocked down.

'You old stumblebum!' he cried. Big Boy squealed with pleasure and wrapped his trunk around Roger's neck in a choking embrace. A crowd gathered like magic. Everybody was happy because Roger was happy.

Everybody but Chief Mumbo.

'My son?' he said. 'My son did not come with him?'

All eyes turned to the forest. There was no sign of little Bo. Only the elephant had escaped from the black-birders' camp. With the remarkable homing instinct possessed by so many mammals and birds, he had found his way back to Roger.

He was somewhat the worse for wear. His hide bore several bruises where he had perhaps been kicked by the heavy boots of the Thunder-man or beaten with sticks. He was well muddied by his journey and Roger took him into the lake for a bath, scrubbing his hide all over, particularly behind the ears and in any cracks or folds where ticks had attached themselves.

Then boy and beast came out, both trumpeting, and Big Boy was served a breakfast of milk, milk, and more milk. He put away so much of it that it was plain he must have been half starved in the camp of the black-birders.

They must be punished. Bo must be rescued. But how

could their camp be found? It would do no good to follow the blackbirders' tracks.

But how about the tracks of Big Boy? That was it. Full of sudden enthusiasm, he proposed the idea to Joro.

Joro nodded thoughtfully.

'Maybe good,' Joro said. 'Maybe good.'

So when the expedition started out, it ignored the foot prints of the night visitors and followed those of the baby elephant. The idea had been Roger's, but the tracking was Joro's, and he performed it with great skill. Even when the trail was confused by the prints of other ele phantine feet, including those of the young, Joro was able to pick out the footprints of Big Boy.

They led to Green Lake, but did not vanish in the water. Instead, they followed the shore, not toward Beego Bog, but to the right, round the east end of the lake, then past the waterfall and up the steep slope to the next terrace or balcony, where Black Lake sulked under heavy clouds. Here were giant palms, giant mimosa and grass eight feet high. A super-size rhino was feeding on a super-size nettle, munching the three-inch-long spikes of the nettle with as much pleasure as if they had been so much ice cream and cake. Mammoth groundsels flowered along the edge of the lake.

It was all so unreal that Roger said, 'I must be dream ing.'

'Your dream takes you back about three million years,' Hal said. 'This is the way it was at that time over much of Africa. Down on the Serengeti Plain not far from here archaeologists have discovered the fossil remains of giant pigs, giant sheep, giant ostriches, a tremendous baboon, and a rhino twice as large as the ones to be found there today. Africa was a land of giants. Now the giants are gone – except in these mountains.'

'I still don't quite understand,' Roger said, 'why the giants disappeared everywhere else but stayed on here.'

'Nobody has come up with a good answer to that one. Of course, the daily rain has a lot to do with it. That makes the plants grow, and where there is plenty to eat the animals grow too. But that's not the whole story. Perhaps part of the answer is that this is a sort of island shut away from the world. People are destructive – but few people have ever found their way here. Then there's something about the soil. They say that because this region has never been ripped up by volcanic action it has had the same kind of soil for ages. Anyhow, no matter what the reason, here you are living three million years ago. How does it feel?'

'Spooky,' said Roger.

The heavy fog turned into drizzle, and the drizzle into rain, and the rain into a cloudburst thundering down with such force that in ten minutes the tracks of the baby elephant were completely wiped out.

The rain suddenly stopped. The men came together and looked in vain for more tracks. From the unseen mountains came a last ripple of thunder like a giant's laugh.

Joro ordered the men to make a circle about a hundred feet in diameter around the spot where he stood and examine every inch of ground. They did so, gradually working their way in to the centre. They found nothing. They sat down on the damp ground.

Again came that rumbling chuckle from the hidden mountains.

'Are you going to stay here and be laughed at?' demanded Hal. 'You are men, not children. Those you look

for, they also are only men, not gods. You don't need
to be afraid of them. They must be somewhere – they
can't vanish into thin air. We can find them. Let us break
up into teams – two men in each team. Each team will go
out from this point in a different direction like the spokes
of a wheel. We will go over this country with a fine-tooth
comb. At noon we will come back to this place and tell
what we have seen.'

The men shook their heads wearily and muttered under
their breath, but they obeyed. Joro appointed the teams.
Each team set out towards a different point of the com-
pass, except back to camp. Hal and Roger, constituting
a team, started due north.

Their route took them up another steep slope among
monster plants with hairy arms and flowers that looked
like daisies but were as big as dinner plates. Moss which
should have been nothing more than a soft carpet under
their feet stood as high as Roger's head. They fought
their way through it for a few yards and then stopped.

'This isn't going to work,' Hal said. 'It would take us
all day to go a mile through this stuff.'

'How do the animals get through it?' Roger asked.

'That's a good question. If we can just get the answer
we'll be in business. The answer may be tunnels. Let's go
back and start again.'

They struggled back to the beginning of the moss and
followed the edge. They found tunnels, but they were too
small – probably made by snakes or rodents.

'I think I could wriggle through this one,' Roger said.

'And run the chance of meeting a cobra face to face.
We can do better than that.'

A bush pig suddenly dashed out of a larger tunnel in
the moss thicket, then stopped abruptly when it saw the

two boys. It snorted angrily and seemed quite ready t
make trouble. Its tusks looked as sharp as knives.

'Just stand still,' Hal advised.

The big boar glared and grunted and made a few fals
starts towards these strangers who had invaded h
domain. But when they did not stir he decided to gi
them the cold shoulder. With a final snort and a toss
his head he plunged on down the mountain-side.

23 | The tunnel

THEY peered into the tunnel. It was about three feet high and two wide. It was as dark as a coal cellar.

Roger didn't like the look of it. 'We'd have to go through on our hands and knees,' he objected. 'And suppose we met another bush pig. It's so dark – anything might happen in there.'

'Just keep in mind,' Hal said, 'that a bush pig probably doesn't like it any better than you do. He never knows when he might meet a leopard or something equally unpleasant. So if you hear a grunt, just grunt back. I'm sure you're as good a grunter as any bush pig.'

'Thanks for the compliment,' Roger said. 'But just in case a grunt doesn't stop him, I'll have my knife handy.'

'In your teeth,' Hal suggested. 'You'll need your hands for crawling.'

Down on all fours, with long knives clenched between their teeth, the two looked savage enough to terrify a bush pig.

Hal led the way into the tunnel. If there was any trouble ahead, he would be the one to meet it. This made Roger feel better – until it occurred to him that the trouble might come from behind.

In that case *he* would be the one to suffer. And if he were attacked from behind, how could he use his knife? The tunnel was too tight a fit to allow him to turn round.

He had thought Hal was quite brave to go ahead. Now he wasn't so sure. Hal was guarded by a knife in front and a knife behind. Roger was protected in front, but his rear began to twitch and itch with quivering fear of the sharp tusks of a bush pig or the claws or jaws of a leopard. And there was nothing he could do about it.

'Okay?' Hal said. His voice had a muffled sound, deadened by the moss.

'Okay,' Roger replied.

But now he had a new worry. Who could tell how long this tunnel might be? It might go on for miles and miles. The twigs and stones on the floor of the tunnel were already punching into his hands and knees. How much of this sort of thing could he stand?

Again Hal called but his voice, smothered in moss, was fainter now. Roger shouted back.

He crawled on for several minutes. Suddenly he butted his head against a solid column of moss. He stopped and explored with his hands. He found that the tunnel forked at this point and became two tunnels.

Now what? Which one had his brother followed?

'Hal!' he shouted. His voice sounded as if his mouth were full of feathers. The moss choked the sound. He heard no reply. He shouted again, and heard nothing.

Why hadn't Hal waited for him? Probably because he hadn't noticed the fork. Roger wouldn't have noticed it himself if he hadn't happened to bump into the moss between the two passages. Roger tried to be calm and think this thing out reasonably. If Hal had not noticed the fork he would naturally have gone straight ahead. Now, which direction was straight ahead?

That was hard to tell in complete darkness. The two tunnels were both nearly straight ahead.

His heart was beating like a trip hammer. He tried to tell himself that this was just because of the altitude. After all, they were far up the slope of a high mountain. And crawling on hands and knees took a good deal of energy.

But he didn't fool himself. He knew the chief reason for his fast pulse and rapid breathing was that he was scared. He felt like a mouse in a trap.

He didn't enjoy being all alone in this black hole, and still he was afraid he was not alone – who could tell what things with tusks or claws or poisonous fangs might be waiting in the dark? If he could only see where he was and where to go!

He slashed at the ceiling with his knife. The stout rope-like branches of moss were intertwined in a solid mass. He kept cutting and sawing and slashing until his arm was lame. Then he caught a glimmer of light through the roof. He kept up the attack until he had made a hole large enough for his head to pass through.

It was a good feeling to get his head out. But all he saw was moss, moss, and more moss. On every side it was visible for only a little way and then was swallowed by the fog.

He was even more uncertain of direction than he had been down below. There he had at least a choice between two tunnels.

He drew in his head and plunged into the tunnel that bore to the right. He called again. No answer. No use wasting his breath calling. On sore hands and knees he hurried along, expecting to lay his fingers on the smooth round body of a snake at any moment.

Presently he came to another meeting of tunnels. Here

he could turn either right or left. It was all the same to him. He turned left.

Soon he stopped to listen. There was a rustling somewhere ahead of him. Something was coming.

He hoped it was something small and harmless, perhaps a hedgehog or a hare. No, a small animal would not make so much noise. The scraping against walls and roof told him it was something almost as large as the tunnel.

Swiftly, his mind pictured the possibilities. The thing could be a gorilla, or a giant ant-bear, or a hyena. It could be a bush pig or a wart-hog, and either one of these mean beasts carried razer-edged tusks.

Worst of all, it could be a leopard. The thought paralysed him. Perhaps he should try to back up. But a leopard could come forward faster than he could go backward.

Besides, if he showed fear the leopard was sure to attack him. He must put on a brave front.

He remembered what his brother had said about grunting. He would do better than that – he would roar.

Roar he did, and no leopard could have roared better. At the same time he charged. His only hope was to scare this beast, and make it back down.

A terrific roar answered him. Roger tried to top this roar with one that almost burst his lungs. He scrambled ahead as fast as his hand and knees would carry him, giving roar for roar.

His head crashed against the head of his enemy.

'Ouch!' said the leopard.

'Ouch!' said Roger.

The two leopards sat down on their haunches and laughed. It was a nervous laugh, for they had both been thoroughly frightened.

'Imagine meeting *you* here,' said Hal.

'Why didn't you wait for me at the fork?'

'Was there a fork? Now I'll ask you a question – how come you're going the wrong way?'

'I got mixed up on a detour.'

'Can you turn around?'

Roger tried it. He squirmed and twisted and gave it up. 'No,' he said. 'This tunnel is too tight a fit.'

'Then you'll just have to crawl backwards the rest of the way. Don't worry. It can't be more than five or ten miles.'

'You're so funny,' Roger groaned. 'I'll bet I can turn round in five minutes.'

'If you can, you're more of a magician than I take you for.'

Roger crawled backwards until he reached the side tunnel from which he had come. He backed into it and waited for Hal to pass him. Then he fell in quietly behind his brother.

Hal, supposing Roger to be still in front of him, was startled by a savage growl behind him and the prick of a leopard's claw in his rear – then he realized it was just the point of Roger's knife.

'You scared me out of my skin,' he admitted. 'How did you get there?'

'Easy,' Roger said. 'It's just as you say – I'm more of a magician than you take me for.'

Wearily they crawled on for another hour. Then Hal stopped to rest.

'I've been on my hands and knees so long,' he said, 'I don't believe I'll ever be able to stand up on my hind feet again.'

Roger lay flat on the ground. 'I'm going to take a nap.

You'll find me here when you come back.'

But the sound of small things, perhaps snaky things creeping through the moss, was enough to keep him awake. Presently he found himself shivering.

'I'm getting cold. Let's get a move on.'

'Seems to me there's a cold draught,' Hal said as he started forward. 'Perhaps we're getting near the end of this thing. Look – isn't that a spot of daylight ahead?'

They crawled with new energy, the spot of light grew and they came out at last into a glare that made them blink. There was no sun, but they had been so long in the dark that even the white pillars of fog drifting round them hurt their eyes. A cold wind was blowing. Roger hunched his shoulders.

'Hey, I thought we were on the Equator.'

'So we are, almost. But we're up mighty high, higher than the highest of the Alps.'

Roger stared at him unbelievingly. 'Aren't you laying it on a bit thick? Mont Blanc is over fifteen thousand feet.'

'I know. But these mountains nearly reach seventeen thousand. And we're about sixteen thousand up right now.'

'That makes us real mountain climbers,' Roger said. 'No wonder it's cold. Still there must have been a forest fire or something up here to make these ashes all over the ground.'

'Ashes? You must have fog in your eyes. Put your hand in the ashes.'

Roger did so and came up with a hand covered by a moist white substance.

'Snow!' he exclaimed. 'Snow on the Equator!'

'And look yonder. There's White Lake.'

The rolling mist revealed the lake, and it was truly white, iced from shore to shore, and the ice covered by a thin film of snow.

The landscape was rocky and bare. The giant flowers and monstrous trees had been left behind. Somewhere behind the curtain of fog the ice-covered peaks punctured the sky, and river of ice – the glaciers – crawled down the ravines.

Between billows of fog they could catch glimpses of the wonderland below them – grim Black Lake on its terrace, and on the balcony below that the very beautiful Green Lake glowing like a precious stone and surrounded by extravagant jungle.

Far, far down at the foot of the mountain they could make out the roofs of the small hotel where they had seen a guest book containing the names of famous men who had climbed or tried to climb these peaks. Roger remembered the signatures of princes, counts, and dukes, explorers of the Royal Geographical Society, and Americans such as Lowell Thomas Jr. and Adlai Stevenson.

The remarkable thing was not how many names there were, but how few. The hundreds of thousands of visitors to Africa came and went without even reaching the foot of this most fantastic of all fantastic mountain ranges.

Then the grey curtains came together again and blotted out the lakes and the forests of gigantic flowers, stranger than anything on the moon after which these mountains had been named.

24 | The white elephant

T H E wind-blown fog was constantly changing, taking o
weird shapes, like pillars or trees or shadowy men a hun
dred feet tall.

'It gives me the creeps,' Roger said. 'See that thing
I know it's just fog, but it looks like a white elephant.'

Hal stared at the strange object. It did not act like fo;
If it were fog it would change its shape or drift with th
wind or melt away. But it stayed put and it still looke
like a white elephant, or at least a grey one.

Hal rubbed his eyes. It was still there. Exciteme
began to stir in his veins.

It couldn't be true. White elephants were extreme
rare. The Tokyo Zoo had offered his father fifty thousan
dollars for a white elephant. His father had replied tha
he couldn't guarantee delivery because the chance of fin
ing such an animal was very small.

But Hal had dreamed about it. The dream was alway
the same. He saw a white elephant but, as he came nea
it, it turned into mist and floated away. Perhaps he wa
dreaming now.

'Let's see if it's real,' he said. 'Come on – just one ste
at a time.'

They advanced, step by step. The monster did not mel
It stood its ground without fear, and also without ange

rhaps it had never seen men before and knew no reason
hy it should worry about them.

As they came closer Hal could see that much of the
ok of whiteness was due to the fog. But he had seen
her elephants in the fog and they had not looked as
hite as this one. The hide now seemed a light grey. He
asn't disturbed by this fact because he knew that none
the so-called white elephants in all history have been
ow-white. They were albinos – and an albino is simply
animal without the usual amount of dark colour in the
in.

If he could get close enough he could tell whether this
e was really an albino. There were certain things to look
r. He stepped very carefully, his finger over his mouth.

Roger moved just as quietly. He knew what it was all
out – they had discussed the Tokyo offer many times
d had studied the subject so that they would know an
bino when they saw one.

The great animal continued to regard them with mild
terest. They crept to within ten feet, then stopped.

It was a moment they would never forget – for now
ey were sure, and the thrill almost choked them. The
l-tale marks of the albino could be plainly seen.

The light-grey hide was splashed here and there with a
arm pink as if glowing in the light of a rising sun. A
finite sign of the albino was the white hair along the
ick, like snow on a mountain-top. Other reliable signs
ere the white toe-nails, and the pinkish-white eyes.
lashes of pink tinged the forehead and ears. There was
doubt about it – this was a genuine albino and a real
auty.

Another proof was the mild disposition of the animal.
he albino is usually good-natured. Hal thought of the

white rhinos in Murchison National Park – they were n[ot]
irritable and dangerous like most rhinos. White rabbit[s]
white mice, and the albino birds are all inclined to [be]
friendly. Snow leopards are not feared by man. But blac[k]
leopards and black jaguars are dreaded.

Any zoo that got this white elephant would be fortu[n]-
ate. It would certainly be the leading attraction in t[he]
zoo. Most zoos could not or would not afford it. A[ll]
animal hunters knew that the Japanese were now payi[ng]
the highest prices for rare animals.

And yet the amount they had offered for a white el[e]-
phant was not the highest ever paid. P. T. Barnum, t[he]
great showman, had paid two hundred thousand dolla[rs]

or a white elephant. It was valued so highly because it was the first ever brought to America. To the boys, the offer of fifty thousand dollars made to their father for a white elephant seemed a great fortune.

Here they stood within ten feet of this rich prize and they were helpless. Two boys alone could not take an elephant. They would need every man in their safari, and even then they might fail. All they could do now was to retreat quietly so as not to alarm the beast, and come back as soon as possible with all their men.

They backed away cautiously, step by step, keeping their eyes on the big beauty.

A gruff voice behind them made them turn.

Six men clad in long white Arab burnouses and armed with pistols and sabres faced them.

'We'd better make a run for it,' Roger said under his breath.

'No use,' Hal said. 'They'd shoot us down. We'd better talk with them.' He addressed the man who seemed to be their leader. 'Do you speak English?'

He got no reply except an angry shake of the head and a storm of words in Arabic. Their faces were as Joro had described them, neither white nor black. Their skin was deeply browned by the sun of their desert homeland. Their heads were topped with twisted turbans, but their feet were bare. They did not seem to mind the light snow underfoot and they looked hardy and tough and mean.

As they talked they looked at the white elephant, then at the boys, and back at the elephant.

Hal did not need an interpreter to guess what was on their minds.

'They're probably some of the men who have been looting our camp,' he said 'They know we're after elephants. And so are they. They stole two of ours – and I'll bet they'll do their best to keep us from getting this one.'

'Let's pretend we don't want it.'

'Sure. We'll just give them a polite goodbye and go on our way – if they'll let us.'

But politeness didn't pay off. The moment the boys began to move away they were surrounded and the muzzles of pistols were poked into their ribs. There was ripping of cloth and their eyes were blindfolded. They were aware that their knives were being drawn from their belts. Then they were harshly jabbed in the back and made to march.

Every time they stumbled over stones or hummocks
ey got an angry scolding and the prick of a steel blade
tween the shoulders.

'If they want us to walk fast,' Roger complained, 'why
n't they let us see where we're going?'

'I suppose they're taking us to their camp. And they
ant to keep its location secret.'

'There's one good thing about it,' Roger said. 'We'll
e Bo – unless he's already been sent away. Perhaps we
n even rescue him.'

Hal did not answer. He liked his brother's courage, but
thought Roger did not realize how serious the situa-
n was. Two boys at the mercy of a gang of cut-throats
re not likely to rescue anybody, even themselves.

It was hard going. They were already pretty well fagged
t by the long crawl up the mountain-side through the
oss tunnel. They were hungry. But at least they were
t cold. A chill wind was blowing from the eternal
ows. But there was something about staggering along
th the point of a sabre in your back that kept you warm.

At first they were pushed round in a circle. That was to
nfuse them completely so they would not know one
rection from another.

But there was one thing the blackbirders had not taken
to account: the wind. Hal had noticed day after day
at the prevailing wind was from west to east. Now,
hen they finished circling and took a fairly straight
urse, the wind was on their backs. Hal salted this fact
vay in his memory. If they ever made their escape from
e robber band they should go against the wind. That
ould bring them back to White Lake, and from there
ey knew their way down past Black Lake and Green
ke to their own camp.

That could be a useful bit of knowledge *if* the
escaped. It was a large 'if'.

After a march of possibly two hours they heard voice
ahead. Then suddenly the wind left their backs and so di
the sabres. The air was warm and there was a smell of fir
and of cooking.

The bandages were yanked from their faces.

They stood in a great cave lighted by splutterin
torches and warmed by open wood fires. Stalactites hun
like crystal chandeliers from the ceiling, the walls wer
covered with rich draperies and the ground was carpete
with the yellow-and-black skins of leopards. Men in lon
white robes took their ease on the black-and-gold skins
using leopards' heads as arm-rests. The aromatic smell o
mint rose from the glasses of tea with which they re
freshed themselves.

'A scene right out of *The Arabian Nights*,' Hal re
marked.

'Or the palace of Monte Cristo,' Roger added.

5 | The thunder-man

'I A M glad you like it.'

The voice was so deep that it seemed to have come om the rock walls of the cavern itself. The boys turned arply to see who had spoken.

They faced a huge man taller than Hal and as thick rough as two Hals. He was not dressed in the sort of hite burnous worn by the other men. Instead, his long be was a rainbow of rich colours and was made of the nest silk that softly reflected the light of the torches. A reast plate fashioned in gold and silver and set with leaming jewels covered his chest. Instead of a turban he ore a head-dress fashioned from the mane of a lion. A now leopard had died to provide his splendid belt, and the belt were thrust a large ornamental pistol and a cimitar in a scabbard of cloth-of-gold. His feet were ncased in finely embroidered slippers twice ordinary ze and the boys were reminded of the huge boot-prints ft near their camp when Bo and the elephants were olen.

There could be no doubt about it – this was the chief of e blackbirders, the one whom the Watussi called the hunder-man.

But just now there was no thundercloud in the face of e Thunder-man. He smiled, and his teeth looked even

whiter than they were in contrast with the deep copp
colour of his face. He bowed.

'It is kind of you to visit our humble quarters,' he sai
'You must be in need of refreshment. Please follow me

Hal burned with the things he wanted to say, thin
that were not too pleasant, but this did not seem to be t
time to say them.

The Thunder-man held aside a brocaded curtain an
they passed into a smaller cavern even more sumptuous
adorned. Thick cushions lay on the leopard-skin carpe
The robber chief flung himself down among them, an
Hal and Roger, weary from their long ordeal, were gla
to do the same. An attendant came in with a tray bearin
three glasses of hot mint tea and some cakes.

'I trust you will like our tea,' said the big man. 'I am
sorry we have no coffee. I came to like it during my
travels in Western countries. But when I am at home I
prefer the old ways.'

'And this is your home?'

'No, no,' laughed the Thunder-man. 'This is just a
camp. I am sheik over some fifty thousand people on the
shore of the Persian Gulf. The oil from our lands makes
your automobiles run and enriches us. But I am not con-
tent to be a stay-at-home sheik. I have a taste for adventure – so, for a part of the year, I leave a palace to live in
a cave, and I appoint others to enforce the law among my
people while I have the pleasure of breaking the law
here.'

'So you admit you are breaking the law?'

'Of course. Why should I try to hide from you what
you already know very well? We have made many visits
to your camp. The village of your Watussi friends has
provided us with many handsome slaves. Where we send
them, they are warmly received and bring a good price.'

'You took the chief's son,' Hal said. 'Has he been sent
away?'

'No, he is still with us. Would you like to see him?'

Without waiting for an answer he clapped his hands
and when an attendant entered he gave an order in
Arabic.

A moment later the curtains parted and there was Bo.
He exclaimed with pleasure when he saw the boys and
ran forward to take their hands.

'How good that you have come! I knew you would
come for me. I knew it.'

'It isn't quite that way,' Hal said regretfully. 'We are
prisoners. I'm afraid we won't be of much help to you.'

The pleasure faded from Bo's face.

'I am sorry – for you,' he said. 'This sheik who giv
you smiles and tea and cakes and cushions – he has mu
der in his heart. I warn you. Do not trust him.'

A roar of laughter from the sheik interrupted Bo.

'This boy – I like him. He has spirit. No one else dar
to speak before me in this way. He is a chief's son – an
he speaks like a chief.'

His face darkened and a savage fury came into his eye
He went on:

'But I will teach him better manners. He has had som
lessons already. Turn about, boy, let us see your back.'

Bo did not move.

The Thunder-man gave a sharp order in Arabic. A
attendant seized Bo and spun him about so that his bac
could be seen. The skin was striped with swollen ridge
some of them still bleeding. The Thunder-man was smi
ing. Roger said hotly:

'Why don't you pick on someone your own size, yc
big bully? I suppose you'll keep this up until you k
him.'

'Kill him? Certainly not, my friend. I kill nothing th:
is worth good money. He will make a fine slave – but h
spirit must be broken first. Just the way you would brea
in a horse.'

'Is it necessary to be so brutal about it?' Hal said.

'Brutal? How can you say that? We are really ver
gentle. Let me show you what we use.'

He took down from the wall an innocent-looking str
of leather.

'Feel it,' he said. 'See how soft it is. In our countr
we have a name for it – in English it would be "so
persuasion".'

'You know better than that,' Hal said. 'This is one of
the cruellest weapons man ever made. In South Africa it
is called a sjambok. It's made of rhino hide and it is
softened with lion fat. It is not made soft so that it will
not hurt – is is made soft so that it *will* hurt. It is so
pliable that every inch of it sinks into the flesh. It is used
as a whip and it will cut like a knife. Any man who
would order a boy to be whipped with this thing deserves
to feel it on his own back.'

The Thunder-man's eyes flashed, but he still smiled.

'I'm afraid you do not set a good example for your
young friend. You are as impertinent as he is. Imperti-
nence must be punished.' He threw the whip to an attendant who pushed Bo out between the curtains. 'Perhaps
twenty more lashes on his back will make all of you a
little more respectful. It will be done just outside the
curtains so that we will all have the pleasure of hearing
him howl.'

At the first stroke of the whip Roger leaped up. Hal
pulled him down again.

'We're only making things worse for Bo,' he said. 'Lie
low. Our chance will come.'

The sheik was plainly disappointed when the twenty
lashes brought no howl out of Bo, nor any other sound
great or small. Hal and Roger gritted their teeth and felt
every blow as if it had been on their own backs. When it
was all over the sheik said:

'So much for him. Now for you. Perhaps you wonder
why you have been brought here.'

'Do you expect to make slaves of us?' Hal inquired.

'I'm afraid no one would buy you. My friends are very
particular. They don't like the smell of white people.
White slaves are hard to teach. They are always trying

to escape. And your government might give us trouble.
No, I fear the easy life of a slave in a millionaire's
mansion is not for you. You can't expect to be so lucky.'

'Then why do you hold us?'

'I have no objection to telling you why. Today you
found a white elephant. My men saw you. They know
that you are after animals and there is no animal in all
Africa, nor in all the world, half so valuable as a white
elephant. You and your men would have tried to take
that elephant. We had to stop you.'

'Why should you want a white elephant? You can't
turn it into a slave.'

'True. But in a certain land of the Far East I can sell
that animal for the price of ten Cadillacs. We must hold
you until we have captured and sold that elephant.'

'And what do you suppose our men will be doing in
the meantime? They will search for us, and find this
place. They are many and you are few. You will lose your
lives and your elephant too. Is an elephant worth all that
risk? After all, an elephant is only an elephant.'

The Thunder-man smiled his mean smile.

'You can't pull the wool over my eyes, young man. I
have been in Burma and Siam – some call it Thailand but
I prefer Siam. I have made a little study of this matter of
white elephants. Let me tell you what I saw in the court
of Siam.

'A white elephant was housed in a magnificent pavil-
ion. It was robed in elegant silks trimmed with scarlet,
silver, white, and gold. On its tusks were bands of solid
gold. Over its head was the royal umbrella.

'A hundred nobles waited upon it. Some cooled it with
fans of ostrich plumes, some brushed the flies away, some
fed it rare fruits from vessels of gold.

'When it was taken to the river to bathe a canopy of cloth-of-gold was carried over it by eight men. Musicians marched before it playing instruments. When it came from the river a mandarin washed its feet in a silver basin and annointed them with sweet perfumes.'

'But why all this fuss over a mere animal?'

'To them it is not a mere animal. It is a Buddha, a god, and the common people worship it. When it dies the ceremonies are the same as those for a king or queen. The body lies in state for several days. Then it is cremated on a funeral pyre made of the finest sandal, sassafras, and other precious woods, and costing thousands of dollars. The ashes are collected, put in costly urns, and buried in the royal cemetery.

'In former times it was believed that the earth was supported on the back of a white elephant, and whenever it moved an earthquake was produced. And did you ever hear about the present the King of Siam sent to Queen Victoria? It was in a gold box locked with a gold key. Everyone thought it must be a very rich gem since it came in so fine a box. They opened the box. It contained a few hairs from the king's white elephant. This was the most precious gift the Siamese king could think of to present to the Queen. And when the Siamese ambassador wanted to say something very nice about Queen Victoria he said, "Her eyes, complexion, and, above all, her bearing, are those of a beautiful and majestic white elephant." '

'But the King of Siam already has several white elephants,' Hal objected. 'Why should he want another?'

'Because he has only Siamese elephants. The African elephant is bigger, taller, several tons heavier, has greater ears and longer tusks, and is a more majestic animal in

every way.' The Thunder-man rose. 'And that, my friends
is why the animal you saw today is about to make a little
journey to the royal court of Siam. Until this is accomplished, you will be our guests. And I must warn you
that if you interfere with our plans in any way you will
not go from this place alive. Good night, and pleasant
dreams.'

E clapped his hands. Guards appeared instantly. The
boys rose and were led out of the Thunder-man's apart-
ment and back through the great cave, which was now
almost completely dark and empty. From smaller caves
behind curtains, evidently sleeping-rooms, came the
snores of men already asleep and the subdued voices of
those who were not.

At the rear of the main cavern they entered a small
cave where the smell of mint tea was especially strong. A
large pot of the stuff steamed gently over a small wood
fire. The place was feebly lit by the sputtering light of a
single torch. There were no comforts here, no leopard-
skin carpet, no cushions. The walls were bare rock, the
ground cold and stony. In one corner was a sleeping,
bare-skinned figure, huddled into a ball to keep warm.
The voices of the guards made it stir and turn. Then it
stood up and the boys realized it was the son of Chief
Mumbo.

'Bo!' exclaimed Roger, going to him. 'What kind of a
dump is this they keep you in? A fine place for a Watussi
prince.'

Bo smiled weakly. 'Slave quarters,' he said. 'This is
their prison until they are sent away. The others went
yesterday to meet a dhow that will take them to some

Red Sea port. They tell me I go tomorrow – bound for
some place on the Persian Gulf.'

Roger looked about. 'It's worse than a dungeon,' he
said. 'A dungeon usually has at least one tiny window.
This has none.' He looked at the steaming pot. 'At least
you get tea.'

'That's for the guards,' Bo replied. 'To keep them
awake.'

'What do they give you to eat?'

'Nothing,' Bo said. 'Nothing at all. They say they will
give me food when I get down on my knees and ask for it.
I won't do that. They say I can't be a good slave until I
forget that I am the son of a chief. They say they will
starve me until I forget. They may starve me until I die,
but I will not forget.'

Hal thought as he looked at the proud young figure
holding himself straight in spite of the pain he must feel
from the deep cuts that had been laid upon his back.
There's good stuff in this boy. He will make a great chief
– if he has the chance.

But Bo would never have the chance if he were
whisked away tomorrow to a life of slavery. If Hal could
do anything to save him it must be done now, tonight.

Hal's eye travelled over every inch of the wall, roof, and
ground of the dungeon. There was not a sign of any opening, except the entrance from the main cavern. This was
completely blocked by six guards. Three of them sat
wedged together in the doorway and three just inside.
Bundled up in their burnouses, the tails of which were
tucked under them to protect them from the cold ground,
they drank tea and conversed in low tones. They were
big men, and well armed with pistols and sabres.

Only one guard with a pistol would be enough to pre-

ent the escape of unarmed prisoners. What chance had
three boys, without weapons, against six armed men?

Even if the six had nothing to fight with, their shouts
would bring other men at the run.

Of course they would shout – but, for the sake of argument, suppose they did not. Suppose that, by some
miracle, the boys were able to defeat the guards, silently,
and get through into the main cavern. They would still
have to go down the length of the great cavern between
the small sleeping-caves to get outside. Not everybody
would be sound asleep. Some would be sure to poke out
their heads to see what was going on. They would raise a
cry and the boys would promptly be captured.

It all seemed quite hopeless. Hal gave it up. He rolled
over on his side, intending to get some sleep.

Something hard in the pocket of his bush jacket
punched into him uncomfortably. He shifted a little to get
the hard thing out from under his hip.

Then he sat up, pop-eyed. This thing in his pocket. It
might do the trick.

He slipped in his hand and felt it – a cartridge about a
half-inch in diameter and three inches long.

It was the sort of thing they often used after noosing a
rhino or other large beast. It contained a sleeping drug
called Sernyl. It could be fitted with a hypodermic needle
and shot from a crossbow into the animal's hide.

In fifteen minutes the beast would stop kicking and
bucking. He would go to sleep and stay asleep for four
hours, giving the men plenty of opportunity to winch his
body up into a truck, transport him to camp, and haul
him into a cage.

If the contents of one cartridge were enough to dope a
huge rhino or buffalo or elephant, they ought to be quite

enough to put six men, or even a dozen men, soun
asleep.

But how could he get the stuff into the guards? He ha
no crossbow, nor more than one cartridge, and even
he had he could not imagine that the men would sit sti
and allow him to shoot them.

His eye lit on the great pot of tea on the fire. Th
guards seemed to have an unlimited capacity for te
Every few minutes they refilled their glasses. If he coul
empty the cartridge into the pot . . .

He hunched along the ground a little closer to the fir
All six guards immediately turned their eyes upon hir
He held out his hands towards the hot embers. Th
guards, assuming that he was merely coming closer
the fire in order to get warm, paid no further attention 1
him.

He shifted about slowly until he was between them an
the fire. He waited until the men were deep in convers:
tion. Then he slipped his hand into his pocket and dre
out the cartridge. Hiding it with his body, he removed th
plug and poured the contents into the tea. The emp'
cartridge went back into his pocket.

He moved over to rejoin Roger and Bo. Roger kne
what had happened, and Bo could guess, but neith
gave any sign that would awaken suspicion in th
guards.

Presently the men refilled their glasses and drank. H
was on pins and needles – would they notice a change i
the taste? Luckily the strong mint flavour was enough 1
conceal any slight taste of the drug.

It seemed an eternity, but it could not have been mo
than a quarter of an hour before the conversation lagge
dragged, and then stopped. The heads of the guard

egan to droop. At first they prodded each other awake but soon they all gave in to an overpowering sleepiness nd there was no sound but their heavy breathing.

The three boys edged towards the door. The guards did ot stir. Hal carefully stepped over their bodies and drew side the door-curtain an inch or two so that he could see own the length of the main cavern.

The place was nearly dark. Only a few torches still urned. At first he could see no one – but upon looking ore carefully he made out a few men, apparently asleep, sing leopards' heads as pillows.

Hal whispered to his companions. 'We're in a tough pot. If one of those fellows sees us, the game is up.'

'It's pretty dark out there,' Roger said.

'Not so dark that they can't tell the difference between ur clothes and a white burnous.'

Roger looked down at the sleeping guards. 'Well, what re we waiting for? If it's white burnouses we want, here hey are.'

The bodies were heavy and it took some heaving and ulling to get the burnouses off three of the men. But hen the boys were finally gowned in the long white obes with the hoods drawn over their heads, there was othing but their faces to betray the fact that they were ot blackbirders.

Quietly they stepped out of the dungeon and strolled hrough the cavern. Their hearts were thumping. They ould hardly keep from breaking into a run. But they new they must take it easy and arouse no suspicion. hey passed the first man successfully. They kept their aces turned away, but it was hardly necessary since he emained fast asleep.

The second man raised his head as they came by. All

he saw was three white backs. He rolled over on his side
and closed his eyes.

Very lazily, the three wandered on past a third man
and a fourth. Passing outside, they stopped for a moment
as if they had merely come out to enjoy the fresh air.
Then they wandered to one side, and out of sight.

Now they were suddenly electrified. They picked up
their skirts and ran. Hal led off straight into the wind. It
was not as strong as by day, but enough to give him a
sense of direction. The going was rough. The moon,
glinting through breaks in the eternal fog, was helpful but
not reliable. It had a way of hiding its face just when
there were some rocks in the way. Shins were soon barked
and bleeding, but the race continued.

At long last, White Lake gleamed faintly ahead.

'And there's our white elephant,' exclaimed Roger.

It stood very near the spot where they had first come
upon it.

'But I think I'm seeing double,' said Hal, straining his
eyes. 'Do I see a black elephant too – or is it just the
white one's shadow?'

They crept closer. The misty moonlight brightened for
a moment and they could quite clearly see the second
elephant. Its dark hide proved at once that it was no
albino.

Some patient searching was necessary to re-locate the
moss tunnel.

'Don't much like the idea of diving into that in the
middle of the night,' Roger said.

Hal agreed with him. 'I know what you mean. But after
all, it's just as dark in there in the daytime as at night.'

'So it is. But isn't there more of a chance of leopards
prowling around in there at night?'

'It's a chance we'll have to take. What's bothering me how do we crawl on our hands and knees in these ghtgowns?'

They could throw off the burnouses and leave them hind. That didn't appeal to them, for the air was nip- ng cold. They tucked the clumsy garments up around eir waists as tightly as possible and plunged into the nnel.

The undermoss world was full of small strange noises, t they got through it without encountering anything ore dangerous than a civet cat which was more fright- ed than they were.

Then down past Black Lake and Green Lake and rough the gorilla forest to the camp. Dead tired, they anted nothing more than to drop down on their beds d forget the blackbirders and everything else.

'But there's one thing we must do at once,' Hal said. low that we know where the blackbirders hang out, we n give the police some definite information.'

They woke Bo's father. The chief wept with joy to see s son. He dispatched a runner at once to the police ation of Mutwanga at the foot of the mountain.

The police, grumpy and grouchy because their sleep d been disturbed, did not get on their way up the ountain until mid-morning. Hal met them and led them, ong with his own men, to the cave of the blackbirders. rely so strong a force could overcome the robber nd.

At the head of his little army, Hal marched boldly into e cavern.

It was empty.

The slavers, realizing that their secret hiding-place was w known, had fled. Leopard carpets and all were gone.

Nothing remained but the faint odour of mint tea.

'They were too smart for us,' Hal said in bitter dis
appointment.

The police were annoyed. It had been a stiff climb up
the mountain. They were tired and scratched and bruised
and half frozen. And Hal realized they blamed him for
all their troubles. From their black faces he got black
looks and they mumbled Swahili insults which he luckily
did not understand. But he understood clearly enough
that he could not expect more help from them in bringing
the slavers to justice.

27 | Capture of the white elephant

H E could guess what the robbers would do next. Some of them had seen the white elephant, and the Thunder-man himself had said that he meant to capture it.

'There's no time to lose,' Hal said. 'Of course, they may have grabbed it already, but I think it's hardly likely. They must have been too busy this morning packing and leaving to bother about elephants. We still have a chance.'

They began the return march towards White Lake. Roger plodded along with his head down.

'What's the matter, kid?' Hal inquired. 'Some deep thinking going on?'

Roger looked up, and there was mischief in his eyes.

'Just wondering if we could play a trick on those night-town boys,' he said.

'What kind of a trick?'

Roger explained his plan. Hal grinned.

'It just might work,' he said. 'They tell me there's a short cut from here to our camp. Take one of the police with you – he'll know the way, so you won't have to crawl through that tunnel. You'll have to make a quick trip of it. I can't hold the police long.'

'Okay,' Roger said. 'Big Boy and I will meet you at White Lake in about an hour.'

Roger and his police escort went at a jog-trot down th
mountain-side to the camp. Roger ransacked the suppl
truck, found a spray gun and filled it with white pain
The villagers watched these strange proceedings wit
curiosity, but he told them nothing.

Then he called Big Boy. The baby elephant lumbere
up to him, squealing with pleasure.

'I have a job for you,' Roger said. 'Come along.'

He and his police companion struck out for Whit
Lake. The elephant trundled along behind. It was a har
climb, and fast.

They arrived at the lake shore to find the safari me
waiting patiently and the police impatiently, whil
Hal used all his powers of persuasion to hold ther
steady.

When they saw Roger walk in with a spray gun in hi
hands and a baby elephant at his heels, they were full c
questions. Roger gave them no answers. He peered abou
through the fog, searching for the white elephant.

'Am I in time?' he asked anxiously. 'Did the black
birders get the big white?'

'Not yet,' Hal said. 'But you're not a minute too soo
They're on the way here. We sent out a scout and he ha
just come back with some bad news. They have a lc
more men than we thought. Twice as many as we have
And they're all armed with pistols. Our police have onl
their spears; and our safari men, only knives – excep
Toto.'

Since the Hunt safari was a take-'em-alive outfit, not
shooting safari, usually only one rifle was carried, an
that was now in the hands of Toto, the gunbearer.

'If they come all in a bunch,' Hal went on, 'we can
possibly beat them. But if your paint-pot idea work

maybe we can confuse them and scatter them, and then
pick them off one by one.'

'Well, let's get to it. But where's our white?'

'Over there. Behind those rocks.'

Roger, squinting through the fog, at first could make
out nothing but black-and-white rocks. Then one of the
white 'rocks' moved – and a black 'rock' changed position
and threw up its trunk and screamed.

The boys sneaked up on the black elephant. It saw
them and began to move away. They broke into a run
and reached it in time to spray one flank and then the
other with the white paint.

Now its own mother wouldn't know it. In ten seconds
the black elephant had become a white elephant. It
ambled off, still screaming.

'I hope it goes right on squawking,' Hal said.
'The more it has to say, the more likely they are to
find it.'

Between the blasts of the black elephant, there was a
new sound – the voices of the approaching robbers.

Hal gave some quick orders. He sent half of his men on
the trail of the painted elephant. The others were told to
retreat from the lake shore and hide behind rocks near
the white elephant.

He prayed that the mist would remain thick – thick
enough so that Roger's clever plan would get results.

Perhaps the Mountains of the Moon heard the prayer.
At any rate, they co-operated with the very stickiest and
pea-soupiest of fogs.

Loud shouts in Arabic came through the gloom. Hal
and Roger could guess what was going on and they were
very happy about it. The blackbirders were chasing the
painted elephant.

Now it was time for the white elephant to do her pa
If she would kindly scream, she would distract the ro
bers and some of them would come to investigate. So tl
robber band would be divided and would more easily
overcome.

But the big white was too placid a beast to raise h
voice in a scream. Roger's plan was on the edge
failure.

Hal saved it. Suddenly he let loose with a perfe
elephantine performance, beginning with a deep bello
and running up the scale to a piercing shriek. He follow
it with another, and another.

At once there came the scrambling sound of runni
feet and a blackbirder appeared. The police caught hi
and overpowered him before he could use his pistol. I
was immediately tied hand and foot.

One in the bag!

Another burst through the fog, and was nabbed. Thr
came all at once, and were taken, but one of them h
time to fire his pistol and a policeman fell.

Now they came by the dozen, and the safari men join
the police in overcoming them and tying them up. O
of Hal's best men, Mali, was shot in the arm. He kept
fighting.

'Later,' he said, when Hal offered him first aid.

Roger ran to see how the war was going for the paint
elephant. From behind a rock he watched with glee
the blackbirders bearing down upon the imitation wh
elephant were picked off and bound. Some were eas
caught, for they stood confused, hearing elephant voic
in two directions and not knowing which way to g
Others who got close enough to their quarry to see th
it was really just an ordinary elephant with a coat

aint, stood bewildered, cursing the trick that had been layed upon them.

Suddenly Roger heard a scream that couldn't have ome from Hal's throat.

He ran back to discover that some blackbirders who ad managed to get to the white elephant were pricking with their sabres, to drive it towards their camp, where- ver that might be. The animal responded with screams f pain and anger.

Perhaps these were some of the same men who had ruelly cut off an elephant's trunk so that the enraged east would run wild over the safari camp and the village.

Their brutal methods this time had a result that they ere not expecting. The usually good-natured animal hirled about in sudden fury, stabbed two men with her sks, crushed one under her great forefeet, and flailed out with her trunk, knocking men to the ground at ery sweep. The rest leaped out of her way, only to be abbed by safari men or police.

That clinches it, Hal thought. We've got them licked.

But he had forgotten the Thunder-man.

At one moment Hal was surrounded by drifting pillars fog. At the next moment, one of the pillars became rk and solid and Hal stood face to face with the chief the blackbirders.

The robber sheik smiled his mean smile. 'How very rtunate!' he said. 'You are exactly the person I wanted meet.' He drew his pistol.

'Wait,' Hal said. 'I have no gun. You can shoot me th that thing – but what would that prove? Just that u are a coward. If you are a man, put your gun away. ght me hand to hand.'

The blackbirder slapped the pistol back into its sheath. His smile went black.

'You call a sheik of Araby a coward?'

He hurled his great bulk forward. Taller than Hal, heavier by far, he came on like a runaway locomotive.

At the last instant, Hal stepped aside, used a *judo* flip that he had learned in Japan, and the sheik's great weight and momentum became his own undoing. Instead of being blocked, as he had expected, he was propelled forward even faster.

He tripped, fell, and crashed his great head against a rock. There he lay senseless.

He might recover at any moment. Hal worked fast. He had no rope, and there were no vines to be had. He tore strips from the big man's gaudy burnous and firmly tied him up.

The sheik opened his eyes. He struggled vainly. Through the fog came some of the police, also Toto. The police stepped warily about the trussed-up giant and looked in amazement at Hal.

'They say you must have used white man's magic,' Toto said.

Hal, remembering that he owed his success to an Oriental art, said, 'It was magic all right, but not the white man's.'

While the police with the help of the safari men were getting the defeated slavers together for the march down the mountain on the way to a Congolese prison, Hal and Roger had other business.

Roger's little elephant, Big Boy, had been concealed behind a great rock in the care of one of the men. The little fellow's snorts and squeals had attracted the great white female.

Now the boys found the two elephants together. They were already friends. This was exactly what Roger had hoped for. It was elephant nature. A motherless baby elephant will take to any grown-up, and an adult female elephant will become an 'aunt' to any baby that needs her help. So the two were already nuzzling trunks and talking to each other in throaty gurglings.

When the little one saw Roger he waddled over to the boy and followed him as he started down the mountain.

Now came the acid test. Would the big white come, or not? She now had reason to hate humans, for the sabres of blackbirders had given her pain. Would she guess the difference between her enemies and her friends? Force had failed to take her. Would gentleness succeed?

She stood looking at the departing baby. A hundred yards, two hundred yards, and still she did not move.

Then Big Boy looked back at her and squealed. Even stupid non-elephants like Hal and Roger could understand his language. He was plainly saying, 'Please come with us.'

'Oh very well, if you need me,' was Auntie's plain reply, and she put her big beautiful body in slow motion on the trail of her three new friends.

The trip to camp was accomplished without incident. On the following day the two elephants journeyed aboard a truck to Mombasa, there to await shipment to the Tokyo Zoo. A cable to the zoo had brought a message of appreciation and a promise that the two animals would not be separated. The price of fifty thousand dollars for the white elephant was confirmed and ten thousand dollars guaranteed for Big Boy.

The boys sent this message to their father:

MOUNTAINS OF THE MOON NEARLY HAD US DOWN. FAILED
TO TAKE ANY ELEPHANTS EXCEPT A BABY AND AN ADULT
WHITE. SENDING TO TOKYO ZOO.

John Hunt replied:

DID YOU SAY WHITE? GREATEST PRIZE IN THE WORLD.
CONGRATULATIONS TO THE CONQUERORS OF THE MOUN-
TAINS OF THE MOON.

illard Price 'Adventure' stories are all about
al and Roger and their amazing adventures in
arch of wild animals for the world's zoos. Here
a complete list of the adventures available in
night:

WALTER FARLEY

The world-famous series about the Black Stallion and Alec Ramsey

All these books are available at your local bookshop or newsagent, or can be ordered direct from the publisher. Just tick the titles you want and fill in the form below.

Prices and availability subject to change without notice.

KNIGHT BOOKS, P.O. Box 11, Falmouth, Cornwall.
Please send cheque or postal order, and allow the following for postage and packing:

U.K.—One book 25p plus 10p per copy for each additional book ordered, up to a maximum of £1.05.

B.F.P.O. and EIRE—25p for the first book plus 10p per copy for the next 8 books, thereafter 5p per book.

OTHER OVERSEAS CUSTOMERS—40p for the first book and 1 per copy for each additional book.

Name ....

Address ....

....